FENCED IN

Novels Set On The Prairies

by Frank Sol

Chapter One

Duncan O'Neale looked up from the worn surface of his oak desk and then spun his chair around to face the window and its magnificent view of the Calgary skyline. *Or at least what can be seen of it from a ground floor office,* he thought. There were times that he wished the office was on an upper floor, but rents increased the higher up you went.

There was a soft knock at the door.

"Come in," Duncan called out as he spun his chair around.

Before he could stand up, the door swung open a well-dressed woman, probably mid-thirties, stepped through. "Mister O'Neale, I need your help."

Duncan gave his prospective client a friendly smile. "I assumed as much by your coming here," he said, rising to his feet. *Now that was a terrible opening line.* "I'm Duncan O'Neale." He stepped around the corner of his desk. "What can O'Neale Investigations do for you?"

"Elizabeth Newcastle." She offered her hand for a quick shake. She was tall, elegantly dressed in a long dark blue skirt and jacket over a pale white blouse. Her dark hair was elaborately braided and she had sharp blue eyes. "I'm looking for my brother. He disappeared."

Compared to her, Duncan felt underdressed in his jeans and cotton shirt. "Please, have a seat." He waved her into one of the visitors' chairs and sat back down himself. He pulled a notepad and pen out of a drawer in his desk to take down whatever notes he felt were necessary. "When did he disappear?"

"Thirty years ago."

Duncan quickly revised his guess at her age to being low forties. "That's a long time to wait before you start looking."

"It's a long and upsetting story." Elizabeth set her purse onto the desk. "I was the firstborn in the family. My mother and father were having marital troubles and she decided to get pregnant with another child...to try and save their marriage."

"A common enough plan," Duncan agreed. *And how often had it worked out badly? Two people trapped in a loveless marriage just for the sake of the children?*

"Jefferson was born in October and he vanished from the hospital nursery two days later."

Duncan made some notes on his pad.

"Of course Jennifer—my mother—had the police involved right away. They found no trace of my brother. No one at the hospital saw anything. No one knew anything. He was put to bed by the nurse and he vanished in the middle of the night.

"My parents haunted the police station, but the police found nothing." She twisted the strap of her purse in her hand. "The detective said that most kidnapped babies are found within twenty-four hours."

Duncan nodded his head. "I know. The kidnapper is usually a woman who's desperate for a child. She takes one and then she's eager to show off her new baby. Her friends and neighbours usually know that the woman wasn't pregnant so after they hear about a missing baby, someone contacts the authorities."

"My parents waited and waited, but no such person was ever found. No ransom note was ever received. Every lead was a dead end. The case was eventually declared cold and closed."

"There's not a lot left to hope for after so long."

"I know that, Mister O'Neale. My mother is now very ill. She wants to see her son one last time before she dies."

"I don't want to disappoint you, Miss Newcastle, but after this long it won't be easy to track him down for you." *It will be impossible!* "Guessing how a baby will look after he grows up—"

"My mother has always been somewhat obsessed with finding Jefferson. As you might imagine." Elizabeth reached into her black leather purse. "She's been looking for years. Hoping and never giving up. She came across these articles last year."

Duncan looked at the handful of newspaper clippings his client had put on top of his desk. "Local rancher wins suit against developer." The man in the picture appeared to be in his early thirties, with black hair and a twinkle in his blue eyes. "Rick Graham celebrates the success of his lawsuit against Williams and Sons Development."

"This is a picture of my father when he was young man." Elizabeth handed over a photograph. "Compare him to Rick Graham."

"There's a definite resemblance." Duncan held the two pictures side-by-side. "In the nose and that cleft in the chin."

"And the eyes. My father had that same twinkle in his eyes."

"From just glancing at these two pictures, I'd say there *was* a family resemblance, but then I'm *looking* for one." Duncan paused. "Looks can be deceiving."

"I know, Mister O'Neale. So does my mother. There are tests which can be done, correct?"

"Of course, but you can hardly stop complete strangers on the street and ask them for a blood sample." Duncan licked his lips and leaned back in his chair. "I'll look into the case for you though."

"Thank you." Elizabeth gave him a warm smile. "Thank you so much."

"Let me just make a photocopy of these." Duncan rose to his feet and hurried into the hallway. The receptionist's desk was empty—it was Cathy's day off—and the air conditioner was on the fritz again.

Duncan tapped the computer keys, bringing the machine out of stand-by mode. He powered up the scanner and put the clippings and photographs into the copy tray and waited for the copies to print out.

A silhouette moved behind the frosted window of Alexander O'Neale's office door, but his father did not emerge to see what Duncan was up too.

Maybe he has a client of his own, Duncan thought. He turned back towards his office.

Elizabeth was standing by the window, staring out at the Calgary skyline. She turned around as the door swung open.

"Thank you, Miss Newcastle." Duncan handed her the original articles and photos. "I'll be in touch after I make some inquiries. Discrete ones, of course."

"Of course. Here's my number." She handed him a card of her own, along with a cheque. "If you have any questions, please don't hesitate to call me."

"I'll do that. Thank you." He eyed the cheque, his eyes widening at the amount.

"I trust you will find that sufficient for a retainer?"

"More than sufficient, Miss Newcastle."

"I pay well for good service. I look forward to your call." Elizabeth picked up her purse and walked into the hallway. The door clicked closed behind her.

"So who are you really, Mister Graham?" Duncan spread the clippings and photos across his desk so he could study them again.

His eyes skimmed across the article about Rick winning the lawsuit—it had something to do with the developer wanting to divert a creek—and were drawn instead to one of the man riding a horse at a rodeo. The picture was somewhat grainy, but it certainly showcased his broad shoulders and long, muscled body. One hand was high in the air as he struggled to stay on the bucking steed. His *Stetson* lay in the dirt behind him and dark hair fell across his forehead. The sharp angles of his face were set in deep concentration, yet a glimmer of a smile was twisting his lips.

Damn, but he is good-looking. Heat centred in his lower abdomen, and Duncan could feel himself growing hard in his jeans. He briefly wondered if the hot summer temperature was getting to his brain. Having lived in Alberta all his life, he'd seen lots of cowboys, but none had ever look quite as hunky and as handsome as this guy. *What was it about him?* He had the looks, definitely the sex appeal, yet there was something else about him that Duncan couldn't define.

Duncan picked up another clipping. Rick, wearing a fireman's uniform, carrying a child away from a burning building.

Fireman and cowboy? You really do know to push all of a guy's buttons. Duncan shifted positions, trying to release the pressure in the front of his jeans.

Nothing simple and easy for you, I gather. Duncan had a feeling that Rick thrived on challenges. Handsome, tough, and fearless were the first three words that came to mind. *I bet he's got a winning knack with all the ladies too,* he thought with a touch of bitterness.

Duncan wiped his face with the back of his hand and took a glance at his watch. Even though it was only early afternoon, he decided that he'd had more than enough of the office. *Time to head home and relax.* Not that he'd actually stop working just because he was at home—many days, he got more work done on his home computer than in the office.

Duncan gathered up his hastily-jotted down case notes, the newspaper clippings, and a few other odds into his briefcase and then headed for the door.

The offices which housed O'Neale Investigations consisted of four rooms—a reception area, his father's office and his own, then a small storage room which housed their files.

The door to his father's office swung open and Alexander O'Neale stepped into the hallway. "What the hell is going on?" he snarled. "It's like an oven in here. Why in hell don't you have the air-conditioning turned on?"

Involuntarily, Duncan froze in mid-step and slowly turned around. His father was ex-army, an old soldier who stood over six feet tall and had a hefty frame and a sour disposition. To say they never saw eye-to-eye on anything was an understatement. *But I need someone who won't handle me lightly, someone who offers me a challenge.*

Alexander certainly met those conditions. He even had the sleeves of his shirt rolled up, as if looking for a fight.

Duncan suppressed a quiet sigh. A part of him was still searching for a closer relationship with his father—he felt like he barely knew the man even after twenty-seven years of living with him. *Mom died when I was two and you've never quite forgiven me,* he thought, though after so long there was no surge of emotion attached to the accusation. *I just want to have a normal life and an actual father-son connection.*

Being gay was just one small part of the difficulty.

They'd been partners for two years and Alexander criticized, ridiculed, and browbeat him at every turn. Duncan usually managed to give back as good as he got, but what did that say about him—that he was a glutton for punishment? Or, like Elizabeth Newcastle, was he desperately trying to find a happy ending for a fairy tale?

Duncan gave his father a too-sweet smile. "You're a detective. Can't you figure out why it's so hot in here?"

"Shit. It's out again."

"You got it."

Alexander wiped his arm across his forehead. "Did you call that damn repair man?"

Duncan took a deep breath. "Yes, of course I did. He said he'd be here tomorrow morning."

"Tomorrow morning!" The ear-splitting exclamation almost shook the pictures on the walls. "What the hell's the matter with him?"

"It's July. He's busy."

"You have to learn to push, boy. You're too damn soft. How many times do I have to tell you that?"

Duncan kept his temper in check. "Feel free to push all you want. I'm going home where it's cool."

"He'll have his ass over here by this afternoon." Alexander headed back towards his office, then stopped. He turned back around. "Who was that women I saw leaving?"

Not a girlfriend so don't get your hopes up, dad. "Miss Elizabeth Newcastle. She hired me to find her brother."

"What?" One eyebrow jerked upward in surprise.

"Her brother was stolen from a hospital nursery almost thirty years ago when he was two days old."

"Oh, for crying out loud. Why would you take such a damned fool case? Call her and tell her you've changed your mind. We've already got plenty of work to keep us busy."

"*You* have plenty of work," Duncan argued. "I'm just running errands and finding files for you. You said you didn't trust me with the Goldfarb case."

"It's the high-profile cases which bring in the money, not these damned dead-end ones. Get your head out of the god-damned clouds."

Duncan stiffened his backbone, which took physical effort in the heat. "I have no intention of doing any such thing."

"Don't talk back to me, boy. Just do what I tell you too." Now it was Alexander who sighed loudly. "You never could learn to leave well enough alone. You're too soft-hearted, too quick to let criminals go with just a word of warning instead of throwing their asses in a cell for the night."

"Like you would have done?"

"Scare them straight...it's proven to work."

"Proven by who? Who conducted the tests?"

"Don't go throwing that fancy college learning at me, boy. It made you soft...and being soft is what got you fired from that security firm."

Duncan bit his lip to keep from saying anything.

"You should've been a cop, like me. Then you would have learned the real lessons. A cop learns never to put his heart into any kind of cases, but you had to learn it the hard way."

Duncan gritted his teeth until his jaw ached. "That's what you keep telling me, Dad, but I don't regret any of my decisions." He paused. "Well, maybe the one where I became your partner."

"Assistant. You are my *assistant*." Alexander managed a tight smile. "A *partner* would be helping with the Goldfarb case."

"Well, I won't keep you from your work." Duncan enjoyed seeing his father's momentarily startled expression. "I have my own case to work on."

"It's a mistake, getting involved after so many years. She might think she wants her brother back, but he's never known her. This is only going to end in tragedy."

"It won't."

"It will. For them both...and you'll get dragged through hell right along with them."

"Maybe you're right. Maybe you're wrong, though. Yes, I do tend to get emotionally involved, but I'm older now and much stronger, especially after working with you."

Alexander nodded, taking the words as an actual compliment. "I told you I'd put some grit in your gizzard."

Duncan grimaced. "That sounds very painful. I'd rather have chocolate in my gizzard; it's a whole lot sweeter."

Alexander rolled his eyes.

"Anyway, the case shouldn't be too difficult. Miss Newcastle thinks she's already found her brother. Her mother has some news clippings and the pictures of this guy look like the father did in his youth. I just have to make contact and prove be that this man is or isn't the right man. Very easy case."

"Just make sure it doesn't interfere with our real work."

"I'll do it in my spare time. It's not like I have a social life or a family."

"If you moved out on your own, maybe you would."

"Maybe I should move out then."

"Yeah, maybe you should."

Duncan forced a smile onto his face. "I'll keep apartment hunting in mind then." He stepped through the door and into the open air.

* * *

Duncan negotiated the cross-town afternoon traffic the same way he'd handled his father—with gritted teeth. And a lot of patience.

There seemed to be more cars on the roads every day, and his usual route home was blocked by construction. Duncan hated having to detour—the detour made him miss the highway onramp and he had to circle around several more blocks before he got his next chance.

He grimaced. The detour made him circle through streets he normally tried to avoid—some of the potholes were deep enough to swallow his car—and be tied up at traffic lights he usually managed to avoid.

During one of the those traffic light waits, he heard the wail of sirens.

A pair of fire trucks raced through the intersection. Both the pumper and the ladder truck vanished towards the city's core.

"Well, I missed that light," Duncan grumbled. A bright red *Chevy* pick-up turned the corner and drove past. *He might have been cute,* he thought, *if only I'd seen his face.* The quick glimpse of the driver's profile had gotten had been nice enough.

The light changed and he was able to continue on his way home.

On the bright side of things, the *Ford Focus's* air conditioner was working just fine.

Finally, Duncan pulled off the highway and into the suburb where he and his father lived.

He kept the air on high, only turning it down when he actually started to shiver from the cold. He'd always had a love-hate relationship

Involuntarily, Duncan froze in mid-step and slowly turned around. His father was ex-army, an old soldier who stood over six feet tall and had a hefty frame and a sour disposition. To say they never saw eye-to-eye on anything was an understatement. *But I need someone who won't handle me lightly, someone who offers me a challenge.*

Alexander certainly met those conditions. He even had the sleeves of his shirt rolled up, as if looking for a fight.

Duncan suppressed a quiet sigh. A part of him was still searching for a closer relationship with his father—he felt like he barely knew the man even after twenty-seven years of living with him. *Mom died when I was two and you've never quite forgiven me,* he thought, though after so long there was no surge of emotion attached to the accusation. *I just want to have a normal life and an actual father-son connection.*

Being gay was just one small part of the difficulty.

They'd been partners for two years and Alexander criticized, ridiculed, and browbeat him at every turn. Duncan usually managed to give back as good as he got, but what did that say about him—that he was a glutton for punishment? Or, like Elizabeth Newcastle, was he desperately trying to find a happy ending for a fairy tale?

Duncan gave his father a too-sweet smile. "You're a detective. Can't you figure out why it's so hot in here?"

"Shit. It's out again."

"You got it."

Alexander wiped his arm across his forehead. "Did you call that damn repair man?"

Duncan took a deep breath. "Yes, of course I did. He said he'd be here tomorrow morning."

"Tomorrow morning!" The ear-splitting exclamation almost shook the pictures on the walls. "What the hell's the matter with him?"

"It's July. He's busy."

"You have to learn to push, boy. You're too damn soft. How many times do I have to tell you that?"

Duncan kept his temper in check. "Feel free to push all you want. I'm going home where it's cool."

"He'll have his ass over here by this afternoon." Alexander headed back towards his office, then stopped. He turned back around. "Who was that women I saw leaving?"

Not a girlfriend so don't get your hopes up, dad. "Miss Elizabeth Newcastle. She hired me to find her brother."

"What?" One eyebrow jerked upward in surprise.

"Her brother was stolen from a hospital nursery almost thirty years ago when he was two days old."

"Oh, for crying out loud. Why would you take such a damned fool case? Call her and tell her you've changed your mind. We've already got plenty of work to keep us busy."

"*You* have plenty of work," Duncan argued. "I'm just running errands and finding files for you. You said you didn't trust me with the Goldfarb case."

"It's the high-profile cases which bring in the money, not these damned dead-end ones. Get your head out of the god-damned clouds."

Duncan stiffened his backbone, which took physical effort in the heat. "I have no intention of doing any such thing."

"Don't talk back to me, boy. Just do what I tell you too." Now it was Alexander who sighed loudly. "You never could learn to leave well enough alone. You're too soft-hearted, too quick to let criminals go with just a word of warning instead of throwing their asses in a cell for the night."

"Like you would have done?"

"Scare them straight...it's proven to work."

"Proven by who? Who conducted the tests?"

"Don't go throwing that fancy college learning at me, boy. It made you soft...and being soft is what got you fired from that security firm."

Duncan bit his lip to keep from saying anything.

with the Albertan summers. He loved remembering the heat during the blizzards of winter, but he hated that same heat when it actually enveloped the city for weeks on end.

I need to get away for a weekend, he thought as he turned onto his street. He seldom had any opportunity to get away for a whole weekend—Alexander believed in keeping his nose to the grindstone—but if he could find one, he'd take it.

And maybe I can find someone to take a vacation with, he thought. All his friends were married, though, and had families of their own. *I'm still single and starting to feel my age.* Maybe he should have that made into a bumper sticker for his *Ford. Or, better yet, make that 'single and available'. That would certainly draw attention.*

He turned into the driveway with a smile. Getting out of the *Ford,* he glanced at the rows of brick houses, all built back in the late eighties. The houses all looked similar. His parents had bought this house right after they'd gotten married.

This has been my home for my entire life. But maybe it's time for me to move somewhere else. Maybe he could find the elusive family relationship he was chasing if he didn't actually live with his father.

Placing his briefcase on the hood of his *Ford Focus*, Duncan turned on the lawn sprinkler. He watched the spray for a moment, making sure that the water reached the bedraggled-looking flowerbeds, as well as the wilted grass.

Duncan took care of the yard work. He'd long since learned, and accepted, that his father had a black thumb. The sun beat down on his bare head and after the heat of the morning he did something he hadn't actually done in years.

Duncan ran through the sprinkler, laughing aloud and not caring if the neighbours were watching. It felt really good.

He ran through the spray a few more times.

By the time he entered the house, his skin was almost dry. His shirt and jeans were already damp from sweat so the extra water didn't make any difference. The house's air-conditioning felt wonderful on his wet skin. Pure bliss.

Dropping his briefcase on the kitchen table, he poured himself some juice from the fridge.

* * *

The computer hummed softly.

Duncan had taken a cooling shower, to wash away the sweat and grime of the day, and now he was sprawled out on his bed, in just his boxer shorts. He was laying on his stomach and reading over the information he had printed out about Richard—Rick—Graham. You could find out pretty much anything on the Web.

"Ex-firefighter, now rancher."

Rick had earned a citation for bravery, risking his life to save two young children from a burning house, before his retirement. Now he owned a ranch, like Elizabeth had said. He was single and had never been married.

Staring at Rick's picture, Duncan found that fact more than interesting. *Why is a handsome hunk like that still unattached?* One answer jumped to mind—a subtle tease for him—but he pushed it away. Rick was much too masculine and.... *That means absolutely nothing*, Duncan thought. He kept searching.

Rick's parents—Sarah and Michael Graham—were listed as having died in a car wreck just a few days after his birth and he had then been raised by his paternal grandparents. Thomas, his grandfather had been a soldier in the Canadian Forces during the Second World War, and then a firefighter after he mustered out in the fifties. His grandmother, Claudia, had been an army wife who waited for her husband, keeping house and raising their children, until he had returned home and they had settled down in Calgary.

Nothing about Rick's life looked out of the ordinary, but one thing did catch Duncan's attention.

Jefferson Newcastle had been born just five days after Richard Graham in the same hospital in Calgary.

Could that just be a coincidence? Duncan mulled it over for about thirty minutes, then he knew what he had to do. "I've got Rick Graham's address in Bowness, and somehow, someway, I'm just gonna have to get a DNA sample from him."

Chapter Two

The drive from Calgary to the town of Bowness took less than an hour.

I told Elizabeth that I would handle this case with discretion, Duncan reminded himself, *and that's precisely what I plan to do.* The only problem was that he still wasn't sure exactly how he was going to do that. *I need something for a DNA test. I just have to figure out how to get it.* First though, he would meet up with the man in question—Rick Graham—and then he'd just have to take it from there.

Finding Rick's small ranch wasn't a problem for him—he'd gotten precise directions off of *MapQuest*—and very quickly found himself following a gravel road away from the highway.

Fenced pastures stretched along both his right and left. He saw herds of cattle in two of the fields; the rest were empty. He spotted the occasional farmhouse, set well back from the road, but he didn't see anyone outside.

Duncan rounded a copse of trees and spotted the ranch-style frame house. A pipe fence separated it from the pasture and there were corrals and barns to the right. Everything was quiet, with no signs of activity anywhere.

Duncan parked his *Ford* and got out.

He stood, looking around at the farm for several minutes, then walked up the flagstone walk towards the ranch's front door. There was no doorbell, so he knocked and took a second look around.

The wooden veranda-style porch stretched along the front of the white house. The decorative columns supporting the roof were made from oversized horseshoes. Two wrought-iron chairs with denim cushions flanked a picture window, while a matching swing hung from the rafters further on. Although a few low shrubs grew against the house, the neatly mowed yard showed no signs of flowers or flowerbeds. From all of the telltale signs, this was the home of a bachelor.

Or someone else with a black thumb, Duncan thought as he knocked on the door again.

No one answered.

Duncan sighed. "Nothing is ever as easy as it is in the movies," he muttered aloud. The thought of breaking in crossed his mind. *I could be in and out and in less than two minutes with something with Rick's DNA on it,* he thought. But then he shook his head at the absurd thought. *I'm not quite ready to go to those depths. We'll be professional about this.*

Just as he was about to give up and return to his car, he saw a bright red pickup barrelling its way up the driveway. Duncan smiled to himself. "I just got lucky."

Rick Graham enjoyed hearing the gravel crunch under the tires of his *Ford.* It was one of the sounds he found relaxing...and after sharing his weekly lunch with his grandmother, he needed every bit of relaxation that he could muster.

"Visiting with her is like fighting a prairie wildfire," he muttered crossly. He felt raw, sore, and more than a little dazed.

His parents had died when he was a baby, and his grandparents had raised him, though they had never really understood him back then and the years hadn't made much of a difference. He was always aware that he was a big disappointment to both of them.

At five, I was riding granny's broom around the house and pretending it was a horse. Grandpa took it away and made me use it as a gun. He had lost interest in playing after that—he didn't want a gun, he wanted to ride a horse. *They both wanted me to be a fireman, so I became one. Now I want to be a cowboy, and they don't want me too. Well, Granny doesn't.*

His widowed grandmother, Claudia, invited Rick to have lunch with her and her daughter at least once a week. Aunt Pamela was a great cook and he always enjoyed the meal, but his grandmother had been in one of her moods today. Pamela had a new boyfriend who took her out dancing at the bars several nights a week, which upset Claudia because she was left home alone. She had wanted—no, she had demanded—Rick to tell Pamela how bad this man was for her.

I refused—-hell, I don't even know the man!—and then granny had a seizure. Panic attack, heart attack...God. Claudia had always had health issues and doctors had diagnosed her as having a heart murmur. She's already had one heart attack and I thought she was going to have another one right then and there.

He'd spent the rest of the afternoon in the hospital emergency room and the doctor there had finally said Claudia didn't have a heart attack, just an anxiety attack. In the end, his grandmother had gotten exactly what she'd wanted—Pamela would stay home to take care of her.

"She's getting more and more needy as she gets older," Rick muttered to himself. "I'm gonna have to talk with her about her fears of being alone." Not that he was looking forward to such a talk—the bruises were still too raw from today's confrontation. "I'd have a better chance facing down a wild cattle stampede than winning a conversation with Granny." Claudia had a way of making him feel just like a child again.

Rick frowned as he saw a dark green car parked in his driveway. He didn't recognize it as belonging to any of his friends. Then he saw a young man step off his veranda and walk toward the vehicle. A blond in tan shorts that showed off long, slim legs and a yellow-stripped polo shirt which bared tanned arms. His hair was short and brushed back neatly. His shirt and shorts were snug and bulged in all the right places.

Touchable places.

This day just got a hell of a lot better, Rick thought.

A man and his truck, Duncan thought. *Fire engine red...why am I not surprised?* He smiled as the ex-fireman climbed out of the pickup's cab. It was a sight well worth waiting for.

Tight-fitting blue *Wranglers* moulded themselves to Rick's long legs, a gold belt buckle glistened on a tooled leather belt, a starched blue shirt framed his broad shoulders, and a *Stetson* rested perfectly on his dark head. A tuft of dark hair curled above the last button of his shirt.

Oh my God! Duncan thought as the man approached. *He's gorgeous!* "Mister Graham?"

"Yeah."

"Good day , I'm Duncan O'Neale."

"Hello." Still frowning, Rick gave the man's hand a shake.

Such a firm grip, Duncan thought, feeling the blood rushing to his groin. He tried to tear his eyes away, to change his thoughts before the bulge in his shorts grew too noticeable.

Rick grunted softly, then swallowing in a suddenly dry throat, he released Rick's hand. The other man's skin was soft yet strong. *Just like a lady's,* he thought. The moment he looked into Duncan's brown eyes, he felt something warm rising inside him. *You are a cutie, city-boy.* He could feel a swelling inside his jeans and he tried not to squirm uncomfortably. "What can I do for you, Mister O'Neale?"

Duncan felt his knees go weak at the man's deep voice. *Get a grip on yourself!* he told himself. *You're a grown man, not some love-struck teenager at a concert by the latest boy band.* He found himself staring regardless.

Rick's black hair curled into his collar in an unruly, wanton way. His skin was tanned from the sun, but not harsh or weathered by overexposure.

The heat of the sun was hot, but this sensual type of heat was much hotter. It burned through Duncan's body all the way to his toes and he curled them into his sandals.

Looking at his picture is one thing, but seeing him in the flesh is quite another. Duncan sighed as a sign seemed to blink before his eyes. *Cowboy. Dangerous. Stay away.*

For the first time he was physically attracted to a man just by looking at him. He always thought that type of love-at-first-sight reaction was crazy when his friends—both gay and straight—had giggled about it. Of course, he'd found plenty of men to be handsome, but he'd never sleep with them just because of that. Rick Graham was different. *If he so much as crooks his finger...*he drew in a deep breath. Weak and pliable he wasn't.

"Well, can I help you or not?"

"I'm with O'Neale Investigations." Duncan had decided to forego a false cover stories, and rely on brute honesty. He handed over a business card he pulled out of his pocket. "I've been hired to track down a missing person. I've got a few questions I'd like to ask you."

Rick looked at the card, and then gave the other man a second look. *He's a city-boy, but he's certainly not bad to look at.* "Do you want to come inside, out of the sun?"

"Yes, please."

The house was cool after the heat of being in the sun.

Rick wandered into the living room and automatically picked up the TV remote control and clicked on the news. He dropped down into an overstuffed leather chair and put his cowboy booted feet onto a matching ottoman.

Duncan followed him into the room, feeling a surge of emotion at the lack of reaction he was getting. *I didn't even make a blip on your male radar,* he thought bitterly, *though you've certainly sent my gaydar off the scale.* He could feel his already fragile ego taking a nose dive, and quickly brought his thoughts back to the job he was here to do. *I gotta find something suitable for DNA evidence.*

Rick glanced at him, making note of how Duncan was chewing his lip while trying to think of what to say. *Shy and soft-spoken, are you? If you were a woman, "Nice girl" would be written all over your face,* he thought. *And nice women, or pretty boys, are the type I steer well clear of.* People who wanted commitment, two lives joined forever and a part of his soul in the bargain. *I stick with guys who don't get their hearts all bent out of shape just because I chose to walk away instead of following them into their bedrooms. That's who I am—a walk-away guy.* His best friends, Jerry and Chester, had found true love with the women of their dreams, but he knew that wasn't in the cards for him. *Nesting just isn't in my nature. I'm a risk-taker, a cowboy to the core.*

Duncan cleared his throat. "As I was saying to you outside, I've been hired to find a missing person." He took a seat on the leather couch. *Lots of leather…the sign of a bachelor, or a man with a fetish?*

"So what does that have to do with me?" Rick had muted the news.

"Thirty years ago, a baby named Jefferson Newcastle was kidnapped from the Calgary hospital just two nights after he was born. His parents had the police search for him, but they found nothing."

Rick looked him silently.

"Jennifer Newcastle never gave up hoping that her son would be found, someday, and she's waited thirty years for that reunion." Duncan paused, then licked his lips nervously. "She saw your picture in the papers and she thinks you're her son."

Barking out a laugh, Rick shook his head. "That's quite a story," he said. He wondered how long he had been staring at the private eye and hoped he hadn't been caught out. He could still feel that swelling in his jeans and he tried not to squirm uncomfortably.

Duncan nodded. "I know."

"What makes this Newcastle woman so sure that I'm her missing son? It's been thirty years. You said so yourself."

"She's got pictures. The photo of you in the paper looks just like her husband did when he was younger."

"Impossible." Rick shook his head. "There's no way it's true."

"I know this is a shock—"

"You have no idea, Mister O'Neale."

"I've looked at the pictures—I can bring you copies from my car if you want to see them for yourself." Duncan paused, but the other man just shook his head again. "There is a resemblance in your face to Mister Newcastle."

"A fluke."

"A simple blood test would determine the truth."

"It's a lie."

"The test wouldn't cost you a cent, of course, and it would set a sick woman's mind at ease." Duncan paused. *Or else upset her beyond recovery.*

"Listen up, city-boy. I'm Rick Graham, not this Newcastle guy. I'm not interested in—"

"It's a simple test. Painless."

"No."

"You can say 'no' right now, but think about it. You have my card."

"Listen, Mister O'Neale, cause I'm only gonna say this once." Rick exhaled sharply. "I don't need to think this over. I know *exactly* who my parents were. My grandparents raised me after the accident. There is no mystery about my birth. No mystery at all. *You* have the wrong man."

Duncan chewed on the inside of his lip for a moment. He hadn't quite expected such a strong reaction.

Rick was staring at him, challengingly.

"The resemblance between you and the Newcastles is quite convincing. The photos are—"

"You have the wrong man."

"Prove it. A simple little test would settle this once and for all."

"I'm not Jefferson Newcastle!"

"Are you sure you won't reconsider?"

"No."

"All right then." Duncan stood up, not masking the disappointed look on his face. "It was nice to meet you, Mister Graham."

"And you." *Damn*, Rick thought as he watched Duncan standing. *This guy ain't just cute. He was a real hunk.*

"I really do apologize for interrupting your evening." Duncan glanced at the TV again.

"No problem. Sorry I couldn't be more help, but she's wrong," Rick replied though his attention was on his visitor, instead of the television screen. A tuft of chest hair was showing above the open collar of the man's shirt. Rick pulled himself up sharp. *What's wrong with me? This guy ain't my type. He's just a city-boy, not a rough-and-tumble cowboy.* He turned his attention back to the news.

"May I please use your bathroom before I hit the road again?" Duncan gave a nervous laugh.

"Down the hall to the right." Rick breathed a quiet sigh of relief as his visitor disappeared. *The sooner he's gone, the better.*

Duncan hurried to the bathroom, locked the door, and went to work. It was a decent-sized room, built off the master bedroom judging by the second door. *Not quite the method of obtaining a sample that I had in mind, but I guess I'll just have to improvise.* He scanned the shelves, noting the few toiletries and the carefully folded towels. *Very domesticated, aren't you, Mister Graham?*

He sighed. *What I wouldn't give for a comb or a hairbrush,* he thought in annoyance. *Something with even just a few strands of hair in it.* He managed to suppress a sigh.

He caught sight of his face in the mirror. He looked flushed and more than a little wide-eyed. "Calm down," he told himself. "I'm looking like a drug-addled criminal." He closed his eyes and took a deep breath.

And then another.

Duncan opened his eyes and looked around the bathroom again.

"Toothbrush it is." He picked up the toothbrush, eying the worn bristles. *I hope the lab can get something useful from this.* He pulled a small plastic bag out of his back pocket, he slipped the toothbrush into it, then tucked it back. He flushed the toilet and quickly made his way back to the den.

Rick had his amazing sharp blue eyes focused on the TV and didn't even bother to look up.

"Thank you," Duncan told him.

"Sure," he replied, sparing his guest a brief glance.

Duncan had no other choice but to leave. "You have my card if you change your mind."

Rick said nothing in response.

He could have been friendlier. Duncan fumed about that all the way to his Ford. *He was probably used to having his pick of women, or men, and today he just wasn't interested. Or he wasn't interested in me.* Duncan paused in mid-step. Why did that thought hurt so much?

I have to be honest, right? Duncan started his Ford. *I've invaded his privacy and stolen something from his house, so if I never see him again that would probably be for the best—for both of us.*

He didn't believe it though.

All the way back into Calgary, he knew that he had all the evidence he needed to prove if Rick Graham really was Jefferson Newcastle. "I told Elizabeth the odds of it being true were slim and I still believe that to be the case," he said aloud. But those blue eyes were hard to ignore.

The same eyes he'd seen in the photos of the Newcastle men. And in Elizabeth herself.

From his kitchen window, Rick stood with a cold beer in his hand and watched the private eye drive away. He wasn't sure what that little visit was really all about. "So what was he after then?" He had no idea.

It didn't matter though. He'd never see him again after all.

A smile tugged at his mouth. His buddies would laugh at him. Rick was known as a charmer, a ladies' man around the rodeo circuit. He had never met a woman, or a man, whom he didn't like. Or who didn't like him. *So what held me back with...what the hell did he say his name was?* Duncan O'Neale. That was it. What held him back from getting to know Duncan better?

He walked into the living room and sank back down into his favourite chair. *Maybe I'm getting old,* he thought. *Maybe a nice guy like that isn't on my to-do list.* He paused to take a long swallow from the bottle. *Or maybe my instincts tell me that Duncan deserves better than a walk-away cowboy.*

Rick stared at the business card. The tan piece of paper was plainly visible against the marble tabletop.

"What did you really want, Duncan O'Neale?" Rick took a long swallow from the bottle in his hand. "Are you really looking for a missing baby or were you casing the place?" The lawsuit was over and done, but maybe that developer was looking for some payback. "I cost him a fair bit of change...he might be looking to take some payback from me."

Duncan seemed like a nice enough fellow, but surely he wasn't a hired thug.

Chapter Three

Duncan poured himself a cold drink and returned the plastic bottle to the fridge. He thought about adding something alcoholic to the *Coke Zero*, but decided against it. *I'll be a good boy for now,* he thought. He opened the back door and stepped out onto the deck.

There was just enough of a cool breeze blowing to make being outdoors comfortable. Having shade from the house helped too. The radio was playing softly over the wireless speakers he had installed the previous summer.

Duncan took a long sip from the glass. He eyed the yard, taking note of what he needed to look after later than evening. Watering plants mostly. The breeze played across his chest, further cooling him. He had given himself a sponge bath after getting home and was now relaxing, wearing a thin pair of nylon shorts.

He had dropped by the *LifeWorks* labs on his way back into Calgary, dropping off Rick's toothbrush so that the technicians could try and get viable samples from it.

I'm almost hoping that labs don't get a match, he thought. *If they do, it's gonna screw up Rick's life completely. Thirty years of living a lie. But it's also been thirty years of pain for Jennifer too.*

He went back inside to refill his drink. "It's gotta be done though." He set his glass down on the counter. He picked up the phone and carried it up to his bedroom where he rifled through his briefcase. He pulled out Elizabeth's business card.

"*Hello?*"

"Hi, Elizabeth, it's Duncan O'Neale."

"*Is it him?*" There was no mistaking the eagerness in her voice.

"Well, I stopped by to talk with Rick earlier today."

"*And how did your visit go?*"

"He doesn't believe your story." Duncan paused for a moment. "He thinks you and your mother are both crazy." He left his bedroom and started walking back to the kitchen. "But remember, this is all a huge shock for him, suddenly being told that you're really someone else."

"Oh, I suppose it would be."

"I asked him about consenting to a DNA test. He refused."

"Oh," Elizabeth repeated. *"That's unfortunate."*

That's an understatement, Duncan thought. "Well, I knew you wouldn't want to take *no* for an answer. I borrowed his toothbrush and dropped it off at *LifeWorks* today. With any luck, there'll be enough biological matter on it for the techs to get a workable sample."

"I never imagined you would have to resort to illegal methods."

"Usually, I don't. Either the person agrees wholeheartedly, or else I have a court order."

"So, assuming the techs get their sample...."

"They'll need a sample from you for the comparison. A sample from your mother would work better—it would give a closer match."

"Shall I bring her toothbrush then?" Elizabeth sounded amused at the thought. "Or do you want to stop by and purloin it as well?"

"I'll leave how you supply your samples up to you," Duncan replied. "Bringing some hair would be better, but a blood sample would be the best."

"I think I can arrange that."

"Okay then. Let me give you the address." Duncan waited until she had found a pen and some paper, then he listed the address and phone number for the lab. "Just tell them you're there with a sample for the Newcastle case. Mention it's for Duncan O'Neale and they'll know what to do."

"Thank you, Mister O'Neale. You've been very helpful so far."

"That's what you hired me for." Duncan tried to sound confident. "I'm just trying to meet our contract." *Getting to meet Rick is a nice bonus.*

"I'll get the blood sample down to them tomorrow. Good-bye."

"Good-bye, Elizabeth."

Duncan set the phone back into its cradle and picked up his glass. He opened a cupboard and reached for the bottle of rum. "Come on out, Captain Morgan," he said. "I need some company to share this drink."

* * *

Rick woke up to peace and quiet, like always. That was the way he wanted it. His friends called him a people person because he acted so outgoing during community events, but he was really a loner. He enjoyed the peace and the quiet. *Maybe that has something to do with my age,* he thought

When he was younger, partying was in his blood. The more people around him, the better he liked it. Nowadays, he preferred a more sedate life. He was comfortable with his life choices, but he'd probably always regret the rift with his parents. *At least we tried to work through it as a family.* That was important to him.

Rick finished showering and quickly towelled himself dry. He returned to the bedroom and slipped a clean pair of *Levis* over his boxer shorts, before returning to the bathroom to shave.

After rinsing his razor, he reached for his toothbrush, but it wasn't in its usual spot, hanging in the rack. He glanced towards the floor, wondering if he'd dropped it by accident the night before.

There was no sign of it.

Rick pulled open the vanity drawer, and pawed through the *Band-Aids* and ointments in increasing confusion. His toothbrush had disappeared.

"What the hell?" he muttered as he pawed through the drawer again. He'd had it yesterday when he'd brushed his teeth after getting up, before he'd gone to see his grandmother. That was the last time he'd seen it.

None of his friends had been over, and it wasn't the week for the cleaning company to come around. So what could have happened to it?

"Wait a minute," he growled to himself. "That pretty boy in the *Ford* used my bathroom." Could *he* have taken his toothbrush? *What the hell would he want it for?*" It didn't make any sense, but he was becoming increasingly intrigued. *Why would Duncan O'Neale steal my toothbrush?*

The theft made no sense to him at all.

Rick looked around again, but there was nothing else missing that he could see. His toiletries were undisturbed, as were the shelves of folded towels and facecloths. None of his expensive cologne was missing. He had no prescription medications to steal.

Makes no damn sense, he thought again. With a sigh, he reached for the mouthwash to at least rinse his mouth out.

"Next time I'll be a damn sight more careful who I let use my bathroom," he muttered. It was just a toothbrush, less than three bucks so what did it matter?

Rick gave his head a shake. He'd heard stories from cowboys on the rodeo circuit about fan-girls who would steal a personal item from a cowboy they had a crush. But Duncan was no groupie—he was a private investigator.

Wasn't he?

Rick snorted. "So what the hell is going on?" Pulling his comb from the shelf, he gave his hair a quick straightening, before returning to the bedroom to finish dressing.

He made himself a quick cup of coffee before heading outside to the barn. He saddled his horse, Thunderhead, a thoroughbred quarter horse he'd gotten from Jerry, who raised them.

Riding gave him peace and he enjoyed the movement, the rhythm, the sun on his face, and even the calluses on his hands. He knew exactly who he was—a cowboy.

In control.

Jerry was riding his own side of the fence. "Afternoon."

"Afternoon." Rick tipped his *Stetson.*

Jerry was wearing a dirty *Calgary Flames* baseball cap. "You look tired."

"It was a long day yesterday."

"Tell me about it. Had some trouble with the tractor...couldn't get the bastard to start." Jerry spat into the dust. "Finally got it going, but it took almost the whole day."

"Shit, that tractor's older than you are."

"I know," Jerry chuckled. "Got the young lad riding it now. Let him do the hard work while I take a ride."

Rick nodded his agreement. "Must be handy having those extra hands around the farm."

"Can be. Extra mouths to feed and sass back too," he added.

Rick shrugged.

Both ranchers rode along the fence. There was next to no conversation either. They had been friends for so long that riding in companionable silence was sufficient for them.

Rick reined Thunderhead in as they reached the creek which flowed through both of their properties. *The same one the developer wanted to divert*, he thought.

As soon as his boots touched soil, the toothbrush business nagged at him again. *Why did he take my toothbrush?*

Jerry had dismounted so that his own horse could drink from the creek. He leaned against the fence.

Duncan watched the horses drinking. "I had a private eye come out to my place yesterday."

"Did you now?" Jerry gave him a surprised glance. "What'd he want?"

"He wanted me to agree to some DNA testing."

Jerry laughed loudly. "So you got some girl knocked up, did you? Or at least that's what she claims."

"No, nothing like that." Rick smiled, almost embarrassed that he had mentioned it. "Some crazy woman thinks that I'm her kidnapped baby boy."

"You're a bit old to play that role."

"It was thirty years ago."

Jerry whistled.

"Yeah, like I said she's crazy. The private eye seemed pretty certain I was his man too. Must be as crazy as she."

"Must be."

"I think he stole my toothbrush. Right out of my bathroom."

"What is the world coming too?" Jerry shook his head. "Maybe you should press charges."

"For a dollar store toothbrush? What's the point? Not worth the hassle." Even as Jerry laughed again, suddenly, Duncan wanted to find the pretty city-boy in the *Ford*. This mysterious Duncan O'Neale.

Chapter Four

Duncan lay back in his bed, with just a single sheet covering him. The pillow was cool against his neck. He knew he should be sleeping, but his mind was preoccupied with recalling every moment of his meeting with Rick.

"Just some stuck-up rancher," Duncan muttered softly. "Probably has had a string of lady-loves and a pack of kids he only sees a handful of times a year." Getting involved with him would be a terrible idea. "As bad as when I made the mistake of getting involved with Lou...."

The sun was just touching the horizon when Duncan walked up to the front entrance of the small bungalow. He was wearing a pair of loose blue jeans and a short-sleeved cotton shirt. He knocked on the door.

Duncan licked his lips nervously. "Am I doing the right thing?" he murmured to himself. Lou was his partner—a fellow security guard—and so far they'd only just begun to be sociable outside of work. They'd shared a few drinks at the bar with other colleagues, became friends on *Facebook*, and gone to see a truly horrible good-cop-bad-cop action flick at the theatre.

"And today he sends me a message that I should come over to his house so he can show me something." Duncan sighed. "Has he figured out that I'm gay?" And if so, that meant he'd probably be asking to have a new partner assigned to him on Monday.

"Oh well...I'm here right?" Duncan knocked again.

The solid wood door swung inwards.

Duncan stared, his mouth hanging open.

Lou was standing inside, wearing nothing but a pair of tight black briefs which did nothing except draw attention to his package. "Come in, Duncan." He was grinning widely as he stood and held the door open. "What, are you afraid too? Do you want to call for back-up?" He chuckled in his deep, baritone voice.

"You just caught me off-guard," Duncan told him honestly. "You look so incredibly fucking hot." His partner had a slender body, dark-skinned and hairy. Lou even had a piercing in his right nipple."

"Get your ass in here." Lou let the door swing closed behind Duncan. "I've been thinking about inviting you over for a long time." Lou reached over and let his fingers slide down the front of Duncan's shirt, slowly undoing the buttons, and then finally brushing across the front of his jeans.

Duncan bit his lip to keep from crying out. His cock was already hard and straining to escape from the denim.

Lou grabbed him by his now-open shirt and pulled him close. The two men kissed passionately.

Duncan gasped for air.

"I've been watching you for a while." Lou was still smiling. "I was hoping that you'd be interested."

"Oh, I am." Duncan nodded his head eagerly. "God, am I ever! But no one at the station ever mentioned—"

"They don't know." Lou chuckled again. "No one has ever bothered to ask." He bent in close again, bringing his lips against Duncan's.

Still kissing, Lou directed Duncan into bedroom, and pushed his partner down onto the bed.

"Oh yeah!" Duncan moaned as Lou reached for the front of his jeans and yanked them off. He had lost track of when his sandals had been removed and he didn't care.

Lou stuck his hand inside the front of Duncan's boxer shorts and wrapped his fist around his cock. He started jerking, slowly, and Duncan moaned again in delight. "You like that?"

"Do I ever."

"Then you'll really love it when I do this." Lou ducked his head down.

As the moist lips wrapped about his hard-on, Duncan could not help but cry out.

Lou moved his lips up and down on Duncan's shaft until the other man was gasping out that he was ready to blow. Lou chose that moment to back off, pulling Duncan's boxers down to the floor.

Shivering with pent-up excitement and gasping for breath, Duncan lay back on the bed as Lou climbed on top of him.

Duncan moaned, feeling himself almost overwhelmed by the sensations. He could feel Lou's hairy body brushing against his own. Lou's tongue probed deeply into his mouth. And, most noticeable of all, Lou's throbbing erection pressed through the cotton briefs against his own.

After rubbing together for what seemed like hours, Lou pulled away again. "So, Duncan...have you ever had sex in the great outdoors?"

"No, but I think I'm ready to try."

"Good." Lou smiled back and helped pull Duncan off of the bed. "Come on." Lou led his guest out of the bedroom, through the patio doors which opened out onto the deck. It overlooked the backyard of his house.

Duncan looked around nervously, but a tall privacy fence surrounded the yard and pine trees grew thickly around the deck.

"I like lots of privacy," Lou growled. He slid his black briefs down his muscular legs, finally freeing his hard-on from its confinement.

Duncan stared. Lou had an all-over tan.

"I hate tan lines." Lou shook out an oversized beach towel onto the deck. "Come over here."

Duncan followed, staring at Lou's tight ass. It looked like a perfect ass, straight from some Greek statue. And it was just as hairy as the rest of Lou's body.

As soon as he reached the blanket, Duncan dropped down to his knees and wrapped his own lips around Lou's cock.

He ran the tip of his tongue over the head, and Lou moaned gratefully.

Then Lou put his hands on the back of Duncan's head, helping to guide the other man into swallowing the rest of his cock.

Duncan was lacking in practice and it wasn't easy trying to swallow it. It took him at least three tries before his nose finally brushed up against Lou's pubic hair. But the feeling of the stiff fleshy tube pulsating all the way down his throat made it worth the effort. Finally Duncan pulled himself off Lou's member; it was drenched from his blow job.

"Now turn around." Lou paused while the other man turned and got down on his hands and knees. He licked his index finger, and then shoved it into Duncan's ass.

Duncan moaned loudly at the intrusion.

Lou was smiling more widely now.

"Keep going," Duncan groaned. He felt two fingers penetrate him. It took a little more force, but Lou managed to get them both in, and then the massage began. "Oh God!" he gasped as the fingers were removed. "Don't stop, please!"

"And now we go all the way."

Duncan felt the helmet of Lou's penis start to penetrate his hole. "It's still tight," he gasped. "Go slowly. Please."

"I will." Lou's voice was a low growl. "Slow and gentle...I don't want to hurt you."

Duncan slowly pushed himself on and off until he finally engulfed Lou's cock. When the hard-on penetrated all the way, Duncan screamed louder than ever before. Lou was definitely the biggest he'd ever taken.

After a moment, Lou started to thrust.

Duncan moaned. "Oh my God!"

Lou pumped more quickly. "Take it," he growled.

"I'm going to cum!" Duncan could feel the urge building up inside his balls. "I can't hold it!" He pulled himself off Lou's cock, and turned around.

Kneeling there, Lou was grinning widely.

"Oh God!" Just as Duncan started to cum, Lou wrapped his mouth around his cock. Shot after shot went pouring into his mouth, Lou making appreciative noises.

Duncan was gasping for breath. "Oh my God, that was amazing," he said. Sweat was trickling down his chest.

Lou was grinning. "It ain't over yet." He licked his lips. "Get down." He pushed Duncan flat on his stomach on the beach towel. "It's my turn now." Straddling the other man, Lou plunged his dick back into Duncan's still loose hole. He swayed back and forth, each time pushing into his partner with more force. Lou started grunting, and then he suddenly moaned louder than Duncan had.

Duncan lay back on the towel, feeling the other man cum.

With one final thrust, Lou kept his cock planted in Duncan's ass as far as it could go. He smiled down at the other man.

* * *

Rick Graham lay in bed, tossing and turning for hours, completely unable to get Duncan O'Neale out of his mind. A private investigator—that was the last thing he'd expected to find waiting for him when he came home. But he knew from the start that this city-boy wasn't just a pretty guy out for a good time. He was out to destroy his life.

All right, not him exactly, but his mysterious client.

And all this mess just because he had black hair and blue eyes! He knew who he was. There were no doubts about that.

Abruptly, he sat up in bed as something occurred to him.

Duncan had said the Newcastle woman was desperate. What if she tried to contact his grandmother? Duncan had certainly found him easily enough. How much harder would it be to find his grandmother? Given Claudia's fragile health that shock of these wild accusations could be fatal.

He had to make damned sure that never happened.

* * *

"Hello, is Duncan there?"

"Speaking." Duncan blinked at the digital clock on his nightstand. It was ten minutes after nine, but he felt like he'd barely fallen asleep. "What's up?" He tried—and failed—to stifle a yawn.

"It's Eileen from LifeWorks."

"Oh, hi." Duncan was more awake now. "Do you have the test results already?"

"No, actually, we weren't able to get a clear DNA reading from Mister Graham's toothbrush. We're going to need blood or fresh saliva in order to complete the test."

"Thanks for the update, Eileen. I'll get back to you."

"We did get blood samples from both Elizabeth and Jennifer Newcastle. We should have no trouble confirming a match, if there is one that is."

"That's good to know. I'll see what I can do about convincing Mister Graham to part with a more viable sample. Bye."

Rick hung up the phone, cursing. *Damn. This should have been so easy.* How was he going to get a sample of Duncan's blood or saliva? *Just walk and ask him?* "Hey, Rick, would you spit on me?"

He laughed at the thought. "For all I know, once he realized that I stole his toothbrush, he just might spit on me."

Duncan rolled out of bed and stumbled towards the bathroom. He was naked, but it didn't matter. Only his father was around to see him, and they had both seen each other naked often enough.

"I guess I'll have to go back to the ranch and ask Rick more politely for a sample. I tried to be discreet about this...." Being discreet certainly had its advantages, but the ethics of this whole situation bothered him. *I wanted to make things easy for Elizabeth and Rick, until we knew for sure—that's the only reason I stole the toothbrush.*

"I'll have to do this by the book, like Alexander taught me." That was the only option really. "I'll have to tell Rick Graham the truth." He deserved that much.

Chapter Five

Rick pulled up to his grandmother's apartment just after ten o'clock. He let himself into the building through the backdoor—both he and Pamela had their own complete sets of keys. His boots clicked loudly on the stairs and the floors.

As usual, he ignored the elevator and walked up the four flights of stairs. He found the elevator too slow. *Walking is just as fast, and better exercise.* Not that he was concerned with keeping fit...working his ranch kept him in far better shape than any gym membership could.

He walked along the hallways. He could just faintly hear music playing. *Everyone in here is old and more than half deaf.* He knocked on his granny's door.

No response, but he thought he could hear something rumbling. He pulled the key out of his jeans and unlocked the door.

Pamela was vacuuming the living room carpet. She gave a start when she spotted him. "Oh, you should have knocked!" she scolded him.

"I did."

"Take your boots off. Were you born in a barn?"

Rick froze. *I don't know,* he thought. *I might have been...do you know?* He stooped over and pulled off his boots. "They are clean, you know."

"Cowboys have horses and horses live in barns and cowboys clean those barns," his aunt told him. "And so I have a good idea of exactly what your boots have walked through."

"They *are* clean."

"She's still in bed." Pamela hooked her thumb towards the hallway. "Go and see her. I'll put the kettle on."

"All right." Rick walked through the living room and down the short hallway.

"So you haven't forgotten all about me." Propped up in her bed, his petite grandmother looked pale. Sunlight was creeking through the windows, falling across the canopied bed.

"Of course I haven't forgotten about you." Rick was startled by the sight. Her hair hadn't been made up yet and she wasn't wearing make-up—he couldn't recall the last time he had seen her without having perfect hair and make-up.

"I'm sorry I scared you the other day."

"Don't be."

"How about a kiss then?"

Rick stooped over her and gave her a gentle kiss on her cheek.

She smiled at him as he stepped away from the bed.

"I should have stopped by yesterday. I'm sorry. I got distracted on the ranch and—"

"You have a lot to look after there." Claudia was still smiling faintly at him. "The house and barns. Your animals. I can understand you not having time for a sick old woman."

Pamela hurried into the room, fluffing pillows and straightening the bed linens. "You're not that sick," she said. "Just playing up the act cause she has a handsome young doctor now."

Claudia sniffed.

"Forty-something. Distinguished moustache. Yes, if I wasn't already dating Travis then I might have to book a check-up." Pamela winked at Rick. "A complete full-body check-up."

Rick couldn't help but smile at that.

Claudia sniffed again.

Pamela fluffed her pillows some more.

"Aunt Pamela phoned me yesterday to tell me how you were doing. I offered to come over, but she said that you were sleeping."

"She slipped something into my tea."

Pamela looked back over her shoulder at the sharp comment. "Now why would I do something like that?" she asked as she left the bedroom.

Rick sat down in one of the Queen Anne chairs. He shifted positions. *These are not comfortable chairs.* He held his *Stetson* in his hand, feeling out of place. *Just like I usually feel whenever I'm here,* he thought sheepishly. "How are you today?"

"Much better."

"That's good to hear."

Pamela returned, carrying a tray with two teacups on it. "Here you go, cowboy."

Rick took the cup in his hand. The bone china felt so fragile in his fingers. *As delicate as Granny looks,* he thought as he watched Claudia lift her own teacup towards her mouth.

"What did you put in this?" Claudia demanded.

"Just a touch of honey."

Claudia's eyes narrowed. "No more of those damned sleeping pills?"

"Not in this cup. Would you like me to taste-test it first?"

"Oh, give over." Claudia took a sip. "I don't want to argue today."

"Neither do I. I've got vacuuming still to finish. So you visit with your grandmother and keep her occupied while I slave away and make this pigsty look presentable." Pamela gave Rick a wink. "That cute doctor might make a house call." She walked towards the doorway. "And I don't plan on staying in every night, Mother, so get used to it."

The vacuum rumbled back to life.

Rick eyed the now-closed door, then looked back at the woman laying in the bed.

Claudia had placed her teacup onto the nightstand.

Rick set his hat on the floor beside him. "Granny, you can't expect Aunt Pam to stay here with you every day. She has her own apartment to look after. Her own social life. She enjoys going out with her friends."

"Men friends, you mean."

"Whatever."

"My tramp of a daughter has been married three times now and she has absolutely nothing to show for it. Not like your father. He found a girl and settled down happily with her."

Rick bit his lip. "At least Pamela's happy."

"You'd think she'd appreciate having a proper roof over her head."

"She has one."

"That townhouse is in the wrong part of town. She should give it up. There's plenty of room in here for us both."

Rick took a deep breath, trying not to lose his temper. "Aunt Pam has her own life. She can't give it all up for you."

"You always take her side." Claudia sank farther back into the pillows with a hurt expression on her face.

"It's not about sides, Granny." Rick tried to sound conciliatory. He raked his fingers through his hair. "Tell you what. I'll check in to arranging for someone to stay here with you at night. That way it will be easier for both of you."

"You know you remind me of your father when you do that?"

"What?" Rick was caught off-guard by the question.

"Your father. Michael always ran a hand through his hair when he was agitated. His hair was dark and thick like yours."

Rick frowned. *Usually when he did that, it meant that I was in for one his* character-building *lectures.* He shook the thought from his mind. "Granny, did you hear what I said?"

"I don't want a stranger in my home." She shook her head. "Pawing through my possessions. Reading my mail."

"It wouldn't be like that."

"Why can't you stay with me, Rickie?"

He knew his jaw was hanging open. *A few hours aren't going to kill me,* he told himself guiltily. *Aunt Pam does this day after day.* Guilt was a pretty powerful thing. It turned cowboys into sissies.

"It's not like you have a wife or anything," Claudia said as he continued to hesitate.

He managed not to flinch. *We are not going to start talking about your desire to see your grandchildren before you die,* he thought. "I have a ranch to run. It's very time-consuming."

"I never understood your interest in cows and horses. I thought you would outgrow it. You could go back to firefighting. That was a real job. A hero's job."

He bit his inner lip. "No, Granny, I'm done with that."

"Yes, I see that now."

The silence stretched out between them.

An awkward pause followed.

Claudia took a deep breath. "I am proud of you. Your grandfather was too."

"Really?"

"Of course we were, Rickie. It was just hard for us to accept your lifestyle choices."

"You make it sound like I was into some sort of deviant behaviour." He managed to keep his voice calm. *If you had any real idea about what kind of man I really am....*

She looked directly at him. "Why do you get so angry when we talk?"

"Maybe because you always criticize me."

"Do I? I don't mean to."

Rick had had enough of this conversation. He rose to his feet. "It's after eleven. Aren't you getting up today?"

"In a little while perhaps. Those spells just take so much out of me and some days it's hardly worth getting out of bed."

"Getting upset doesn't help."

"I know. I'm just a lonely old woman."

The guilt burned through him like a wildfire. "I'll come and stay with you when Pamela goes out."

Claudia smiled. "Thank you, Rickie."

Closing his eyes for a moment, he took a deep breath. "But, Granny, we have to talk about your fear of being alone."

She shifted uneasily in the bed. "You know I've never liked to stay by myself and ever since Thomas died, it's only gotten worse."

"Maybe you need to get out more."

"Maybe."

"You should call your friends and get back into the bingo group. You always enjoy playing that."

"I've just been so tired lately."

"Then I should let you rest." Rick gave her another kiss. "I'll visit you tomorrow."

"All right."

Rick stepped into the hallway and let the door close behind him.

Pamela was dusting the china cabinet. "Well?"

"We're both going to be taking turns staying with her."

"For a while." Pamela shook her head. "She's eighty-two...well past time that she learned to amuse herself."

"Time to put her into a home, you mean?"

"She's getting to old to be on her own. Neither of us can stay with every minute of the day." She sighed. "Rickie, these things have to be done."

He bit his lip.

* * *

Duncan looked up from his desk as the soft sound of Bert's cursing echoed through the ventilation system. Given that the repairman had been working on it for two days, it appeared that he was having more problems fixing the air conditioner than he had expected.

Duncan chuckled and logged into his *Facebook* page to see if there was anything new. There wasn't.

"*Sitting in my office, bored,*" he typed into his status.

The phone rang.

"*Even a telemarketer would be interesting right now.*" Duncan picked up the phone, making a mental note to press his father to get a more reliable receptionist hired on to man the front desk. "Hello, O'Neale Investigations. How can we help you?"

"*Hi, would Duncan O'Neale be available?*"

"Speaking." Duncan felt his pulse quicken. *There's no mistaking that deep voice.* "Hello, Mister Graham."

"*I want to talk about that case of yours.*"

"The missing Newcastle baby?"

"*Yep. I want to come in and see those pictures of yours.*"

Duncan felt his heart pound harder. "I'll be here all day if you want to come in. You have my address on the card."

"*I know the building you're in. Would three o'clock be all right?*"

"That would be perfect. I'll be waiting."

"*See you then.*"

"Good bye." Duncan heard the phone click. He leaned back in his chair, his eyes half closed. "This day is getting better and better," he muttered to himself. His hand dropped below his desk to stroke the rapidly hardening lump in the front of his jeans.

* * *

Rick sat in his bright red pickup truck, staring through the windshield at the nondescript office building. *Am I here to set some damn fool woman's mind at ease,* he wondered, *or do I just want to see that cute private dick again?*

He opened his door and let his booted feet drop to the parking lot. He walked towards the office building.

Duncan looked up from his desk as someone knocked on his door. "Come in!" he called out. He glanced at the clock hanging on the wall.

It was shaped like a dragon reaching around an ornate, Gothic-styled face; the clock's hands read three o'clock.

The door swung open and Rick stepped into the office.

Duncan licked his lips, trying to keep the goofy grin off his face as he watched the hunky cowboy walk towards his desk.

Rick was wearing a loose chambray shirt and worn jeans. His cowboy boots were dusty, as was his *Stetson*. The hat was pulled low to hide his eyes, but from the firm set of his jaw, Duncan knew Rick wasn't really all that happy to be there.

"Have a seat." Duncan waved Rick to the visitor's chair. He thought about offering his hand, but wasn't sure if the other man would accept. "I was surprised to get your call this morning."

"Were you?"

"Yes. I was going to call on you later, actually, as I wanted to—"

"Look, Mister O'Neale, I'm rather busy at the moment." Rick's sharp blue eyes blazed from under the brim of his hat. "Things to do with my ranch. Arrangements to make regarding the pastures. Stuff like that."

"Of course, I can imagine how busy you—"

"And I have no time," Rick interrupted, "to waste meeting with people who steal from me."

"If you'll give me a few minutes, I can explain."

Rick nodded his head. "I'm here, ain't I? Start talking." He stared across the desk at Duncan with narrowed eyes.

"Well, I was hired to try and prove—or disprove—that you are Jefferson Newcastle. Like I told you a few days ago, a simple blood test would end the mystery."

"There's no mystery. I'm not this Jefferson Newcastle. Your client is mistaken."

"I wanted to try and be discrete...I didn't want to get you all worked up if the test prove Jennifer's beliefs to be false."

"So you stole my toothbrush?"

"I needed something of yours. I didn't see a comb or hairbrush anywhere around." Duncan smiled somewhat sheepishly. "I didn't really want to go snooping through your bathroom."

"So you're a private dick who doesn't sneak?"

"Yeah."

Rick shook his head. "Now I've heard everything."

"Hairs would have been better than your toothbrush, but I went with what I could find."

"What you could steal."

"I can probably get your toothbrush back from the lab."

"No, thank you."

Duncan put his hand into his jeans' pocket. "I'll happily reimburse you for a new one."

Rick laughed at that. "I can afford to buy my own damned toothbrush," he said, still chuckling. "It was old and worn out anyway."

Duncan didn't say anything.

Rick looked at him. "So what did you find out?"

"Well...the lab couldn't get a decent reading. Not enough genetic material to work with."

"I rinsed it too well."

"Yeah...they're hoping for a blood sample."

"A blood sample."

"They only need a small bit. Jennifer Newcastle has already submitted one of her own. So did her daughter."

"I still want you to know that I think both these women are crazy." Rick shook his head. "This is like having a paternity test done."

Duncan frowned at that comment. "Have you had many of them?"

"A few," Rick admitted. "There's always a few crazy women in the world who think you're their dream-man just because you got your picture in the paper."

"Oh."

"None of them came out true. I've always been really careful with women."

"Always used protection?" Duncan asked.

"Yeah." Rick nodded. *When I used to bother going through the motions with women.* It had been a long time since he picked up a woman at a bar, or anywhere else for that matter. *Not since going out with the rest of the gang after our shifts were over.* His colleagues had spent many hours at the fire house boasting about their conquests.

Duncan was still frowning. The offhand comment about paternity tests had startled him. *How many women have been in your life?* he wondered. *How many women threw themselves at your feet just because you were a firefighter?* He was more than willing to throw himself at Rick's feet. *I do love a man in uniform.*

"I've decided to take the DNA test." Rick tried to ignore the sudden sparkle in Duncan's eyes. There was a tuft of dark chest hair showing in the open collar of Duncan's Polo shirt. He caught himself starring at it—and he felt a swelling in his *Levis.*

"Thank you," Duncan said. "Mrs Newcastle will be very grateful."

"I'm not doing this for Mrs Newcastle."

"Oh."

"And not for myself either. I told you, I know who I am." Rick paused. "I figured if Jennifer found me, then she could find my grandmother. Granny is not well right now and the last thing she needs is to be harassed by some woman who thinks I'm her long lost son."

"I can't imagine the Newcastles doing that."

"You can't, but I can. I mean, it's not like they've hired a private eye to visit my home and steal something of mine to get a DNA sample."

"I did that on my own," Duncan told him. "Elizabeth was very surprised to hear that I'd stolen your toothbrush. She sounded disappointed in me."

"Oh." Rick paused. "Anyway, I don't want my granny involved. I'm gonna give your lab their sample and then we're done. The test will come back negative and I won't have to see you again."

Disappointment flashed across Duncan's face.

Rick rose to his feet and walked towards the door. He was still semi-hard in his jeans, but he refused to stay in the office any longer. "There's no need to contact me with the negative news. Just give Mrs Newcastle the results and we're done."

"Mister Graham—"

"I said, 'we're done', Mister O'Neale." He turned his head around for one last look at Duncan. "I don't want to see you again."

Chapter Six

Rick leaned back against the couch and sighed.

"Damn you, Duncan O'Neale. Why the hell did you have to come into my life?" Things had been so much simpler before this. "Just tease the ladies and play around with the odd guy." He hadn't played around with anyone in months though.

"Another round of disappointment to my parents," he muttered as he swallowed another mouthful of beer. "At least grandpa died before he could find out and Granny is still oblivious."

Grandpa would have blamed my schooling. The old man would never had understood that it wasn't just the attitudes around the campus.

"I've always been gay," Rick said aloud. He had come out, sort of, during his first semester at the University of Alberta. Not being familiar with the campus, he had asked a very handsome-looking blond stud for directions to his classroom.

"I'm going to the same building," the man replied with a friendly smile. "Just follow me."

"Thanks." Rick followed him, pausing slightly so that he could lag behind and a get a real good look at this amazing tight butt in cream-coloured slacks. It was a butt well worth a second look. And a third.

Rick felt his face flush when the guy turned around and caught him staring. The man only smiled and went on to point out some of the campus highlights.

When Rick followed his guide into the classroom he had been looking for, he felt himself blushing again. *What a way to start the year off,* he thought. *First day and I'm already gonna have a reputation.* He slumped into the first empty chair he could see.

The guy he had followed had ignored the room's other empty chairs and walked straight to the front of the classroom. He turned around. "Good morning everyone. My name is Allan."

Rick's mouth fell open. *This was his professor? Shit!*

"I'm surprised, really I even passed that class." Rick opened another bottle and took a long swallow. He'd had trouble later, remembering just what all the class was about. Professor Allan was just far too distracting in his handsome looks. *However, I certainly had no trouble getting up every single Monday, Wednesday, and Friday for that class.* No trouble at all getting up—in every sense of the word.

Of course, it wasn't until later in the fall that things came into the open.

Rick was walking down the sidewalk, from the apartment he shared with another student, towards the campus.

"Hello there, Rick."

Rick slowed and turned his head.

Professor Allan was jogging towards them.

"Good afternoon, Professor." Rick felt his heart start to pound at the sight of his hunky professor in a pair of nylon track pants and a loose tee-shirt.

Allan kept jogging, going past them and up the street.

Rick sighed. *I swear he's shaking his ass just for me!*

Ivan, his roommate, chuckled softly. "I think he's hot for you," he said in his heavy Eastern European accent.

"Don't be a dick," Rick replied. He hoped his buddy was joking about Allan, but he was also hoping that he *wasn't.*

"How many times did Allan seem to be walking down that street at the same time I was?" Rick asked aloud. He had a massive hard-on straining against the front of his jeans and he reached down to unzip himself. He let the hard shaft pop out and grasped it with his hand.

"Seemed like he'd pass by at least twice a week. Like my own personal stalker." In a non-creepy way, he added as he started to stroke the smooth skin of his shaft.

Finally, there'd been the afternoon in late October when Allan had been jogging past. He had stopped dead in his tracks and taken hold of Rick's arm and flashed his truly amazing smile. "You should come over sometime," Allan said. "I've got some music I think you would enjoy."

"I can't believe I actually blushed at that," Rick muttered. He could still feel the heat in his cheeks. "And Allan just laughed and slung an arm over my shoulder." Just those few seconds had been more than enough for him to get instantly hard in his jeans...every bit as hard as he was right then. "I had to drop my books down over my crotch and he just laughed again."

Rick sighed. "And then that Friday he finally did it."

After class, Rick remained in his chair, pretending to jot a few final notes into his binder while the rest of the class scattered to freedom.

Allan said good-bye to the last departing student, then he walked away as the door clicked closed. He stopped beside Rick's desk.

Rick looked up. He could see a fairly sizeable bulge in Allan's navy blue slacks and it was getting bigger. His mouth hung open and he could not help but stare.

"So, do you want to come over to my place or not?" Allan asked him. "Or do you just want to stay here and *talk*?" He smiled and put his right hand on his crotch and slowly rubbed at it.

Rick could see the throbbing outline of his professor's big dick swelling against the material and his face flushed even more. "I've never actually had, er..." He voice broke.

"Just take your time," Allan told him. "There's no need to rush."

Rick reached out and cupped his professor's hard-on.

Allan groaned softly. "Do you like what you see?"

"I'm not sure...until I see more."

"Good answer," he chuckled. "Go for it." He moved his hands to his side and thrust his pelvis forward.

Rick quickly realized that he was going to get to do the unwrapping.

He fumbled with Allan's belt and the top button of his slacks. He didn't see the hook, and he was getting frustrated.

"Take it easy, Rick. We want to have a good time, don't we?"

Rick finally managed to get the zipper undone and Allan's slacks slowly slid down his legs, revealing his navy blue boxer shorts.

Allan pulled up his dark blue polo shirt so that Rick could see a trail of fine blond hair moving up his flat stomach and into a bush of hair on his chest.

"It's a beautiful sight," Rick said in a soft voice.

Allan let his shirt drop and then reached down to pull up his slacks. He zipped them back up, his hard-on still plain to the eye. "Not here," he said, hearing Rick's groan of protest. "But you could join me in my office...."

"Do I ever!" Rick stood up—his own excitement plain to see tenting the front of his blue jeans.

Allan carefully locked the door to his small office and then pulled off his shirt as he walked over to Rick who had taken a seat in one of the two chairs. "I've been wanting to do this for a long time." He casually tossed the shirt onto his desk, then bent down and planted a big wet kiss on Rick's face.

Rick almost pulled away in surprise, before he eagerly grabbed his professor's arms.

Allan's tongue explored his mouth and both men was breathing like bulls in heat. He rubbed Rick's nipples through his thin tee-shirt and they hardened to attention.

Rick gasped, plainly surprised that guys' nipples could feel so good!

Allen pushed Rick back against the chair and took his right nipple in his mouth and sucked and licked. He grinned as he listened to Rick's grunts and moans.

Rick felt ready to cum—and Allan hadn't even touched his dick yet!

Allan moved to the other nipple and Rick was in heaven again. He pulled his handsome face back and looked into his student's eyes. "Are you okay with this? Do you want to stop?"

Rick shook his head. "God no!"

"Good, that was what I wanted to hear." Allan stood back up, and then took Rick's head in his hands and guided his face to his once-again open zipper.

Rick had been far too distracted to notice when Allan had unzipped. He groaned as he his teacher rubbed his crotch all over his face.

"Take it out," Allan told him.

Rick slid his hand into Allan's boxers and felt a hot, thick girth pulsing in his fist. "I never knew dicks could get so hot when they're hard."

Allan laughed. "I've got a lot to teach you then." His shaft was dripping clear fluid and he rubbed some of it all over the head of his dick with a thick index finger and then put it in his mouth. "Do you want to suck on it?"

Rick only nodded, unable to speak.

Allen let his shaft touch Rick's lips.

Rick carefully licked the tip and then took the head into his mouth and started to suck on it like some oversized lollipop.

"Do you want me to show you how to suck cock?"

Rick nodded.

"Pay attention...there'll be a test later." Allan chuckled. He stepped back and help Rick stand up. "Come over and sit on the edge of my desk." Then he slid down Rick jeans and briefs. "Oh yeah, you have a very suckable cock." Allan slowly licked Rick's shaft up and down.

Rick's eyes closed as he felt his professor's fingers massaging his balls. "I had no idea it could feel this good."

"I'm only getting started."

Rick flinched nervously when Allan sucked one ball into his mouth and then began swallowing the other. He pulled back, reflexively.

Allan smiled. "Take it easy, I'm not going to hurt you, Rick. I'd never do that. I am, however, going to drive you wild with pleasure."

Rick sighed at the feelings. He wished he could have lasted longer, but Allan had him so hot that he couldn't stop himself. Rick gasped in shock and unexpectedly exploded into Allan's mouth.

Allan left Rick's hard dick in his mouth, taking all of it, right down to its base and just left it there while he gently sucked. Then, finally, he slid back his head, stood up, and looked down at Rick with his bright eyes. "Did you like that?"

"God, did I ever!" Rick groaned. "I had no idea it could feel like that."

The grin on Allan's face grew even wider. He started stroking his thick hard-on until his face got flushed and his eyes squinted closed. He began to groan and breath heavily.

Rick watched, wide-eyed and worn out.

"I'm cumming," Allan whispered.

"Shit!" Rick didn't get out of the way fast enough as Allan shot his load. Hot cum splashed across his crotch and across the bottom of his tee-shirt.

"Sorry about that."

"It's okay." Rick watched as his professor's hard-on slowly start to soften and he suddenly had the urge to take him in his mouth and drain him like he been. He dropped into a crouch and took Allen's dick deep into his mouth. It was a lot easier when it wasn't so hard.

Chapter Seven

Duncan unpacked the last of his dishes and put them away into the cupboards.

The single bedroom apartment wasn't very big, but the rent was reasonable and the view of the Calgary skyline was quite nice. He was within the city, but not in the congested downtown core.

Hopefully the commute to work won't be as nerve wracking, he thought as he closed the door cupboard door. It would certainly be shorter at least.

He had lucked out into finding the vacancy. One of his Facebook friends was moving out of the province and she had needed someone to take over her lease. His dad had been amazed at how fast he had packed up and moved his stuff out of the house.

Six months to enjoy this place and then we'll see if I can extend the lease in my own name or not. He could always move back in with his father if it fell through...but that was far from the perfect solution.

Duncan walked past the living room balcony doors.

There was a squeal of tires from the parking lot.

Duncan glanced through the window, but he was too late to see the vehicle. "Damned punk kids," he muttered in the best imitation of his father.

* * *

"I think you need a drink." Pamela Whelan walked towards the softly humming fridge. She removed a pitcher from its shelf and then moved across the linoleum to a cupboard.

Rick eyed the glass she slid across the table towards him. "You always said that your homemade lemonade was the solution to any problem."

"Isn't it?" She had poured herself a glass as well and now she sat down across the table from him. "So, drink up and tell your auntie all about your problem."

"Am I that obvious?"

"To me." She nodded. Her hair was hanging loosely around her shoulders today and she was wearing a loose blouse and skirt.

Rick took a sip. It was strong and sour, just the way he enjoyed it best. *Not like one of those pale imitation mixes you get at the grocery store.* He flexed his arms, muscles straining against his tee-shirt. "Well, there's this...it seems that...got some awkward questions...some woman...hell."

Pamela laughed softly. "Not easily explained then."

"No, it's not."

"Women problems?" Pamela sipped her lemonade. "I thought you'd be all past those by now."

Rick shrugged, trying not to look guilty. *You have no idea.*

"You should be settled down by now. Married to a nice girl, with a few kids of your own whom I can spoil rotten. Oh, your granny would love to play the doting great-grandmother."

"I haven't found the right person yet. I'm not even looking."

"No?" Pamela shook her head at him. "You can't go through life alone. I'm certainly not."

Rick couldn't help but smile at that. *She's finished with her third husband for real then.* "Are you and Travis getting serious then?"

"We just go out dancing a few nights a week."

"Five nights a week, according to Granny."

"That was just one time! Anyway, it's usually three nights and now it's only going to be one or two." Pamela sighed. "I am *not* giving up all of my nights to stay home and baby-sit her."

"She can't expect you too."

"Oh, Rickie, yes she can. But it's not going to happen."

Rick chuckled. "You were with my mother when I born, right?" He hadn't anticipated asking his aunt this particular question, but the words just slipped out on their own.

Pamela glanced up for a brief second. "Sure was. Brandon and I had just had a big fight over nothing. I had no qualms about leaving him alone while I went to the hospital with Sarah."

Rick folded his arms across his chest as more questions filled his mind. He could feel his stomach twisting as he thought about the possible answers to those questions. "Were you in the room with her?"

"Of course. Moral support and guidance. Your father went weak at the sight of blood. Damned useless in there." Pamela chuckled. "For a few minutes, we thought he was going to faint on us."

Rick laughed as well. The twisting of his stomach eased slightly. "And after they took me home?"

"That was when they were sideswiped." She sighed, her expression growing mournful. "They'd left you with me that night. It was maybe a week or so later that I flew you out to Nova Scotia to your granny and grandpa."

"I see."

"Your granny had her first heart attack after I told her about your folks. But once she saw you, she felt so much better. Just holding you in her arms brought her back to life. You had a thatch of black hair and beautiful blue eyes just like your father." Pamela gave him a weak smile. "Your grandpa was very happy to have the chance to raise you as well."

Rick grimaced. "But not so much as I grew older."

"Rickie, he was disappointed in some of your education and career choices, but that doesn't mean he wasn't still proud of you."

"Sometimes I'm not so sure about that."

His aunt clicked her tongue at him. "Come with me. I want to show you something."

"Show me what?"

"Something important. Now come on." She led Rick into the living room. "It's in here." She went straight to one of the walnut cabinets and opened a drawer. She pulled out a scrapbook. "Take a look at this."

Rick sat down on the couch. The album showed pictures of him as a child...along with report cards, class assignments. For a long moment he was left speechless.

"Dad was never good at showing his feelings, but you were his grandson and he was proud of you."

Rick stared at the pages.

"Both of your grandparents loved you." She studied him for a moment, her eyes narrowing in confusion. "Why are you thinking of all this now?"

He closed the album. "I've just been thinking about stuff."

She didn't look convinced. "Dad, God rest his soul, was a hard man. He believed his way was the right way and he didn't leave you many choices."

"No, but I guess I was as hard and stubborn as he was."

"Stop worrying about the past." She carried the scrapbook back to the cabinet drawer. "Worry about the future...we just need to find a woman for you."

Rick gave her a cheeky. "I can find plenty of those."

"Rick Graham, you naughty boy." Pamela wagged a finger at him. "I mean a forever kind of love that produces babies and happiness."

All of a sudden Rick saw Duncan O'Neale's face, his soft brown eyes and kissable mouth. "Do you think there's such a thing as real happiness?" he asked his aunt.

"Don't ask me. I've certainly never found it, and believe me, Rickie, I've tried. But you, with that face, that dimple and those gorgeous eyes—a woman is just waiting to worship at your feet."

His mouth twitched. *You have no idea,* he thought. "Not exactly what I had in mind." He stood up. "I'll head back to the ranch. Tell Granny I'll call her later."

Pamela studied him, her eyes narrowing again. "You know Travis has a friend who has a niece...."

"No. No blind dates." He reached for his hat.

"Suit yourself, cowboy."

Rick walked slowly across the parking lot towards his truck. He felt so much better now. He realized that he had doubts about the damn-fool DNA test, but after talking with his aunt, it was gone. *I am not Jennifer Newcastle's son.*

He turned and glanced back towards the tall apartment building. His aunt's balcony was festooned with overflowing flowerpots—it was easy to spot—but he didn't see her to wave good-bye too.

Movement in another apartment, on the floor directly below his aunt's caught his eye.

Rick blinked and gave his head a shake. "I do have it bad," he muttered aloud. "That guy looked liked that private dick." But why would Duncan be in the same building as his aunt? *And wandering around in just his boxers? Is that meant to be some kind of tease?* Nope, it had to have been his overworked imagination.

Rick climbed into his pickup.

* * *

"Thank you for coming down." Duncan gestured towards a chair. "Have a seat."

Elizabeth Newcastle sat down, setting her purse on top of the desk. She gave him a nervously excited look. "You've gotten the test results back then?"

"Yes...and the lab found a ninety-nine per cent match."

She exhaled sharply.

"I think the results speak for themselves."

"They do indeed."

There was a long moment of silence.

"So when do I get to meet my brother?" Elizabeth finally asked.

"Now *that* is going to be the complicated part."

"Oh?" Elizabeth raised one narrow eyebrow. "And how is meeting my brother going to be complicated? Jefferson and I have the confirmation from the lab that we share the same DNA."

"Yes, but don't forget Rick—Jefferson—has been living his own life for nearly thirty years. He has no memory of ever being a Newcastle. As far as he's concerned, he is a *Graham*."

"But—" With a sigh, she fell silent. Her eyes narrowed as she frowned. "Yes, you're right...I hadn't thought about it from his perspective. I was just thinking that he would be thrilled to have a sister. I never really thought about that...he never knew that he was kidnapped."

Duncan nodded his own head. "It's going to take time for him to come around to his...we can't press him too hard or else...."

"He'll bolt like one of his horses?"

"Pretty much." Duncan nodded. "He has to adjust to this on his own though. We can't fence him in."

* * *

Rick finished filling the trough with water from the hose. He wanted to make sure that his horses had enough to drink, especially given the early summer heat. He scooped up some of the water in his cupped hands and splashed it against his face.

Then he splashed more on his face—it felt that good.

It was too hot to ride right now.

He adjusted his *Stetson* and turned back towards his house. A cold drink would be so nice and refreshing right now. He could go riding later.

A plume of dust was rising from his driveway.

Rick's eyes narrowed as a dark green *Ford Focus* pulled into view. He *knew* that car.

Duncan O'Neale.

What the hell did he want now? Rick stood by the veranda. He didn't want to think about how thinking about Duncan made his heart pound and his cock twitch. *I just want that city-boy gone. Out of my life.*

Duncan climbed out of his car. A white tank top hugged his chest, and was tucked into tight-fitting blue jeans. The sun glistened off his blond hair.

Rick grimaced. He felt his cock twitch again as Duncan walked towards him. He didn't take any pleasure in that reaction. *This guy is bad news,* he told himself. *Real bad news.*

"Mister Graham, may I speak with you, please?"

Rick snorted and planted his hands on his hips. "Look, Mister O'Neale, you and I have nothing more to say to one another. I thought I made that very clear."

"You did, and I'm sorry, but I have to speak with you."

Rick swallowed as he heard the anxious tone in Duncan's voice. "About what?"

Without a word the private eye handed him a piece of paper. "I don't know how else to do this, but these are the DNA results." Duncan paused for a long moment.

Rick stared at him.

Duncan fidgeted uneasily. "Well," he said, after clearing his throat, "from these results, you are Jennifer Newcastle's biological son."

Rick handed the paper back without looking at it. "There's been a mistake," he said.

"I'm sorry, but DNA doesn't lie."

Rick whipped off his hat and slapped it against his leg. "Look, just stay the hell out of my life." He turned away from Duncan, back towards the barn.

"I *am* sorry, Rick."

"Go away!"

"Rick—"

"Get the hell off my ranch, Duncan." Rick closed his mouth so fast his teeth clicked together. He took another step towards the barn. "Just leave me alone."

"I'm sorry, but I can't do that. Jefferson Newcastle was born five days after you in the same hospital and—"

Rick turned around and glared at his unwelcome guest. "That means nothing. My mother had taken me home by then."

"There's a connection, Mister Graham. I feel it and so do you. Don't you want to know the truth?"

"No."

"You're lying. You're a fighter, a survivor and you're not going to rest until you know what happened all those years ago."

"You don't know anything about me."

"I know enough."

Rick sucked in a breath that felt as hot as the summer sun that seared his skin. "Please leave." He took another couple of steps away, and then turned around. "Have you told the Newcastles yet?"

Feeling reluctant, Duncan nodded his head. "Yes, I had a meeting with Elizabeth this morning."

Rick closed his eyes.

"I know this has to be a shock for you."

"You don't know the half of it. I'll be thirty in October and right now you're telling me that my whole life has been a lie." Rick opened his eyes and resettled his *Stetson* on his head. "There's some mistake. I want the test done again."

"Sure. I don't blame you."

That concerned look in Duncan's eyes threw him. *Why does he care about me?* He wasn't the paying client. "I don't want to have any contact with the Newcastles until after the second test."

"All right."

Rick frowned. "You're being very reasonable."

"I want to make this as easy as possible on everyone."

Then you should have never come here in the first place! Rick thought. "Why do you care so much?"

Duncan shrugged. "Like I said, I know it has to be traumatic to have your world turned upside down."

"Are you talking from experience?"

A smile flashed across the private investigator's face. "My world is always upside down. I seem to be hanging on by my fingernails."

"To me, you look like a guy who can cope." Rick's gaze met Duncan's and he realized they were flirting, getting personal—something he didn't want to do. *Back off...this city-boy is bad news!*

"I'm an O'Neale. I'm supposed to have grit in my backbone, according to my father, and in some other places too." Duncan shrugged. "My dad wanted a rough-and-tumble boy and he got a less than macho son, so I've been conditioned to cope with just about anything."

"Could you cope with finding out that you're not an O'Neale?"

A grimace flashed across Duncan's face. "I'd like to think so."

"The second test will settle this."

Duncan didn't say anything.

Chapter Eight

Rick pushed open the door to his grandmother's apartment. "Hello?" he called out.

"Hello, Rickie." Pamela waved at him through the kitchen doorway. "I'm just in here working on dinner."

"Oh." He inhaled deeply. "Smells wonderful."

"Just my famous homemade spaghetti sauce." She gave him a welcoming smile. "And a few loaves of fresh bread. Sit yourself down."

Rick sat down at the table.

"I didn't know you were coming over today." She glanced up from the pot bubbling away on the stove. "You're more than welcome to stay for supper though. There'll be plenty. There always is." She gave the pot a stir with a wooden spoon.

"I didn't plan on stopping in, but I was in town and thought I'd stop in to see how Granny's doing."

"Oh, she's much better. She actually went out to bingo with some of her uppity friends."

"That's good." Rick smiled in honest relief. "At least she's getting out of bed now."

"She's past the need to be coddled by me...now she's gone out to be fussed over by her friends. Do her the world of good too."

Rick nodded his agreement. "You always take good care of her."

"Most of time I do. And sometimes I just want to strangle her." Pamela gave the sauce another stir with a big wooden spoon. "I'd do pretty much anything for her."

Rick shifted uneasily on the chair. *Would you really?* he thought. *Where would you dry the line?* He shook his head to disrupt that line of thought. "I asked about my birth earlier, but I'd like to talk about it again."

Pamela sighed loudly. "What do you want to know this time?"

"You said you were with my mother when I was born."

"Yes, of course I was. And when I wasn't, Michael was with her. Until the accident, of course. And then I took you out east." Her eyes narrowed. "Why are you asking all these questions?"

Rick exhaled. "Because of this." He pulled the folded up paper with his DNA test results out of his jeans pocket and tossed it onto the table.

"What's this?" Pamela picked it up and unfolded it.

Rick took a deep breath. "It's a DNA test saying I'm Jennifer Newcastle's biological son."

"What?" She quickly read the report. "Who's this Jennifer Newcastle?"

"Her son was born a few days after me in the same hospital. He was stolen from the nursery."

"And now she thinks you're her long-lost son?"

"Yeah."

"That's ridiculous." Pamela shook her head. "It's wrong."

"The blood work came back as a positive match."

"Well, it's still wrong!" She snorted loudly. "Someone at the lab made a mistake."

"I was thinking that myself."

"Oh, Rickie, this is part of some scam. She's out to swindle you."

Rick frowned. "I can't see that happening. What would I have that she'd want?"

"Your farm. Your savings. Something. Everything." His aunt threw the paper back onto the table. "It's all a vicious lie!"

"I thought so too," Rick told her. "That's why I'm taking another test. At a different lab."

"Good, that will clear this up." She gave the sauce another vigorous round of stirring.

Rick stared at her back. He could hear her muttering softly, but he couldn't make out the words. "Tell me that I'm Tom and Claudia's grandson." He couldn't keep that desperate plea out of his voice.

She turned back towards him. "Rickie, for heaven's sakes, of course you are."

He knew his aunt well enough to know she was telling the truth. He swallowed hard. "I don't understand any of this."

"I don't, either, but something's not right. Why are these people trying to destroy your life and Cla...oh good Lord!" In a panic, Pamela dropped the wooden spoon onto the floor. "You can't let Mom find out anything about this. It will upset her terribly. She could have another heart attack."

"Don't worry," Rick replied. "I don't plan on telling her anything until another lab runs the test." *And maybe not even then, assuming the results come back correctly.*

Pamela smiled at him. "So let's just put all this behind us then. You will stay for supper?"

"Yeah, I can't pass up your spaghetti sauce."

"Good boy." Pamela smiled at him. "Now hand me some paper towels to wipe up this mess." She shook her head. "That sauce will stain the floor for sure."

* * *

Duncan looked at the open folder on his desk and sighed.

His father had taken on two new cases—cheating spouses—and tossed them both to his son while he worked on the 'bread winners' as he termed the harder, more public cases.

Duncan sighed again. The two cases were similar—a woman who was allegedly cheating on her husband, and a husband who might be fooling around on his wife—and time-consuming for him. *I'd rather be doing something else,* he thought.

"Why do some people rush out and get married?" he asked aloud. There certainly didn't seem to be very many happy endings to that story. The divorce rate was high and there were always a steady creek of people wanting to get track of what their spouses were doing after work. "Isn't everyone looking for a little happiness?"

And straight people worried that legalizing gay marriage legal was going to bring down society.

"Maybe they're afraid that we're gonna get it right." Duncan laughed somewhat bitterly at that. "Not that I'm seeing anyone right now."

Love at first sight, or so the fairy tales claimed.

Lust at first sight, more truthfully. And those who fell quickly into lust, seemed to fall just as quickly out of it.

Happiness seemed to be a very elusive thing for most people.

Taking a sip of a can of *Coke Zero*—now lukewarm from having sat on the desk for too long—Duncan flipped through his notes.

He had the routine down for the potential cheater-husband. Barry Sherwood worked one of Calgary's largest insurance companies. He left the building just after five o'clock every day. He drove to a local bar and ordered bourbon and water. He watch the news and chat with a few of the other regular patrons. After one drink, he left the bar and went straight home. On those nights in which he claimed to be working late, he was actually working.

Duncan sighed. In his experience, this situation was very rare. Most of the time the wife's instincts were correct.

He'd already called Violet Sherwood and given her his findings after nearly three weeks of surveillance. She hadn't believed him though, and wanted Duncan to keep watching him.

Duncan shook his head. *It's your money,* he had told her. He was supposed to go watching Barry later that night.

Duncan took another sip of *Coke,* and then flipped through a second set of notes. The other case, sadly, had a completely different outcome. Danielle Iorillo met someone every Monday and Thursday morning at a cheap motel, just outside the city. They'd spend several hours together, and then she'd get back into her car and leave.

Duncan had followed her several times. After her two kids had caught the bus to school, she'd drive to the motel. She'd park her car, walk to one of the doors and knock. It would open and she would go inside. Three hours or so would pass, before she would come back out. Afterwards, Danielle would do her shopping or other errands before going back home in time to greet the kids when they got off the school bus.

Duncan always hated to reveal this kind of information, especially when children were involved. But it was what he was paid to do. He looked at Mario's phone number, but he wasn't sure he was ready to make this particular phone call.

"I can't wait forever either," he told himself. "Mario deserves to know the truth." Reluctantly, he reached for the phone and dialled. After three rings, the answering machine kicked on and Duncan sat through the greeting. "Hi, Mario, it's Duncan O'Neale. I've got the information you asked about. Give me a call when you get it." He hung up.

While Duncan completed typing up the file—and making yet another mental note about needing to hire a proper receptionist—Rick was never far from his mind. Every day he had waited for the lab to call and confirm the results. He was still waiting.

The phone rang.

He reached for the receiver. "Hello, O'Neale Investigations. How can we help you?"

"Hello Duncan, it's Elizabeth."

"Oh hi. How are you doing?"

"As well as can be expected. It's been two weeks after all."

"I know." Duncan's eyes flicked towards the calendar hanging on the wall. "I haven't heard anything yet."

"Shouldn't we have heard something by now? The first lab seemed to be much faster."

"I'm afraid that I'm not familiar with this second laboratory. They might very be a bit slower at processing things. They will call as soon as they have the results."

"Are you sure they will? My brother might have asked them not to call us."

"He won't have done that." Actually, Duncan wasn't sure of any such thing. "I'll give them a call later this afternoon though."

"Thank you, Mister O'Neale."

"I'll be in touch, Elizabeth. Good-bye." Duncan hung up.

* * *

Rick Graham climbed into the cab of his red pickup and closed the door. He didn't hear the solid clunk it made.

The folder with the test results was clenched in his hand.

Ninety-nine point nine match.

That didn't leave any room for error. That's what the lab technician had told him. He was Jennifer Newcastle's biological son.

Two separate tests at two different labs. The same results.

Rick drew in a deep breath—it was sharp and painful, like swallowing a fishbone.

I'm not Sarah and Michael's son, he thought. *Claudia and Thomas are not my grandparents.*

He slammed his empty hand against the steering wheel.

Numbly, he gazed out at the summer day. The sky was a brilliant blue and a lone oak tree took pride of place in a small courtyard to the side of the clinic. A woman and her two kids were sitting on a stone bench, probably waiting for someone in the twelve-story building. He saw them, but he didn't really see them. All his thoughts were chaotic and disturbed. He was at the crossroads of his life and what he did now would set the pattern for the years ahead. Of those two things he was certain.

He ran his hand over the steering wheel and then hit it again with his fist. "Shit!" he swore.

Taking a deep breath, Rick threw the folder onto the passenger seat. He was not going to let this rip him apart. He was stronger than that.

"I survived having that building fall on me," he muttered. Sure, he been left with cracked ribs and a broken collarbone. He was an ex-fireman and he had survived burns, broken bones, and even a concussion.

"I'll survive this."

A man emerged from the clinic and the two children rushed from the bench towards him. They latched on his legs.

Rick inhaled deeply, trying to calm his conflicting emotions.

The DNA test had given one answer and created more questions.

What had really happened all those years ago? How had Jennifer Newcastle's newborn baby end up with Claudia Graham?

For a brief moment, he thought about asking that city-boy private investigator, Duncan, for help.

"No. I'm not gonna involve him in this." Rick started up his truck. He thought about calling his friends.

Starting the engine, he thought about calling his buddy, Jerry. Or Stevie. The pair of them had lived through heartache, pain, and family tragedy...and so would he. "No, I can handle this alone."

That meant that his first course of action would be to confront his grandmother.

He took another deep breath. *This ain't gonna be easy.*

As he drove across town to her apartment, Rick kept thinking about he would handle the questioning. With her fragile health, he would have to be delicate.

"But I need answers," he told himself firmly, "and she's got them."

Chapter Nine

Duncan hung up the phone and then slumped back in his chair.

How is he taking it?

The second lab had just phoned with the results of the second DNA test and the samples matched up again.

Elizabeth will be thrilled by this. And Rick...oh, poor Rick.

Duncan sighed again. He felt responsible for the whole mess, even though he was only doing his job. Mrs Newcastle had already found out about Rick Graham and if Duncan had turned down the case, another investigator would have taken it. Maybe his father was right and he was too soft-hearted.

He would give Rick some time before he tried contacting him. By tomorrow, though, he had to let Elizabeth know the results. He couldn't put it off for very much longer.

Alex opened the door walked into the office. "I'm going to put a steak on the grill tonight. You want to stop by for supper?"

"Yeah," Duncan replied, surprised at this offer.

"I'll put another steak on then. See you at home."

Duncan frowned as the door closed, wondering if the heat was getting to Alex. He didn't seem like his father at all.

Poor Rick, he thought, *your life is changing faster than you can adapt.*

* * *

When Rick arrived, Pamela and his granny were eating dinner together.

"Rick, what a pleasant surprise." Pamela had a big, welcoming smile on her face. "Have you had dinner yet?"

"No. I'm not hungry, but I'll take a cup of tea."

Pamela stood up from the table, her eyes focussed on Rick. The message in them was quite clear—don't upset your granny.

"How have you been?" he asked, taking a seat and removing his *Stetson*.

"Much better. I've decided to start playing bridge again."

"That's good. You need to get out more."

Pamela set the porcelain tea cup down in front of him, her eyes watching him like a hawk. He ignored her.

"Did you stop by for a reason, darling?"

"Yes. I'd like to talk about something."

Pamela cleared her throat rather loudly.

"Are you okay?" Claudia asked, staring at Pamela.

"Yes, of course I am," she replied in a soft voice, though her eyes were still shooting daggers towards Rick. "I just don't want you to get upset."

"Upset? Why would I get upset talking to my grandson?" Claudia glanced from him to Pamela. "Do you know what Rick wants to talk about?"

"I'm not sure," Pamela replied in a coldly neutral tone.

"Mother, do you know Jennifer Newcastle?"

Pamela hissed.

Claudia thought for a minute. "No. The name doesn't sound familiar."

"Rick..."

Rick held up a hand, stopping Pamela. "I am your grandson. I believe that."

Claudia's eyes narrowed in obvious confusion. "Of course you are. Why you think any differently?"

He pulled the paper with the DNA results from his shirt pocket and unfolded it. "I'm going to show you something and I want you to stay calm. We can talk about this. Okay?"

"Okay."

He laid the paper in front of her and saw that his hand shook slightly. His hands never shook, not even when he'd heard babies screaming from inside burning houses. He swallowed hard, forcing down his weakness. "This paper says that I'm Jennifer Newcastle's biological son."

"Don't be ridiculous." Claudia brushed the paper away with a nervous laugh.

"I thought it was insane at first, too. But I've taken two different DNA tests and both came back with the exact same results."

"You are Michael's son. Go look at your father's picture. You look just like him."

"I know, but DNA doesn't lie."

"In this case it does." Claudia rose to her feet, her cheeks bright with colour. "I don't know why this Newcastle person is trying to steal my son, but she has the wrong man. You are Rick Graham."

"Granny..."

"I don't care what that test says. You're my grandson. I raised you. I'm not talking about this anymore." Without another word, she walked to her bedroom and quietly closed the door.

Pamela lifted an eyebrow. "She took that very well."

"A little too well," Rick said. *And I don't know what to make of it*. He expected anger and resentment, not calmness.

"Just forget about that Newcastle woman," Pamela suggested. "You're not a baby anymore."

"I know, but someone stole her baby from the hospital. How did that baby end up with Sarah?"

"I don't believe it."

Rick tapped the DNA papers with his finger. "This says otherwise."

Pamela shrugged. "None of this makes any sense."

"Yes, especially since Jefferson Newcastle was born five days before me. There was no way the babies could have been switched in the nursery. That wouldn't make any sense since the Newcastle baby was missing and the Graham baby had already gone home."

"As I said, just forget about it."

He reached for his hat. "Sorry. I can't do that."

"Rick..."

He wasn't listening. He was already out the door.

* * *

Duncan made up a small Caesar salad to go with the steak and baked potatoes which his father was barbequing. He knew Alex wouldn't touch the salad, but he wanted to have one.

Alex brought the platter into the kitchen. Duncan had already set the table, opened a beer for his father and poured himself some juice.

They began eating.

Cutting into his steak, Duncan noted that his father was ignoring the salad. *No surprise there.* "You remember the missing baby case I was working on?"

"Sure I do. A complete waste of time," Alex replied around a mouthful of food.

"No, it wasn't. The man Mrs Newcastle believed was her son really is her biological son."

Alex stopped chewing. "You got to be kidding."

"No."

Alex took a swallow of his beer. "How old is this man?"

"He'll be thirty in October."

"Why in the hell does the Newcastle woman want to tear apart his life now?"

Duncan blinked at the harsh tone. "Because someone stole her baby and she has to know that he's alive and well."

"Doesn't she realize what she's doing to his life?"

"Dad, losing a baby is a traumatic thing, something a woman never gets over. Even though Jennifer Newcastle was able to go on with her life, her missing son was always at the back of her mind. That's why Rick Graham's photo in the paper triggered her hope again. The need to see him is never going away."

Alex snorted. "You should not have gotten yourself involved in this. Once you get emotionally involved in a case, everything goes to hell."

"So I got involved. I admit it. I'm more sensitive than you are."

"You get that from your mother."

Duncan's jaw dropped open. His father never talked about Joan. "Mom was sensitive and caring?"

"Damn right. Waterworks was a regular display and when it was that time of the month, hell, I stayed out of the house."

"Did you ever hold her and tell her you understood?"

His eyebrows knotted together like a rope. "Hell, no, 'cause I didn't understand why every little thing made her cry."

"What did she cry about?" Duncan knew that he might be pressing his luck, but he wanted to hear more.

"When I didn't call and tell her I was going to be late. I was a cop and couldn't call her every few minutes. She cried when I forgot her birthday, and the waterworks lasted a week when I forgot our anniversary."

"She had reasons to cry. That's just plain insensitive."

"But that's me, boy, and you know it. Your mother knew it, too, when she married me. Don't know why she wanted me to be someone I wasn't. Don't know what she saw in me in the first place, but I was so crazy about her that it didn't matter. She was different than I was. Maybe that's why I fell for her. She was this gentle, soft-spoken woman who never saw the bad in anyone."

"Maybe she saw some good in you."

"Could be, but she had to look hard for it."

Duncan was amazed at learning this much. "You never talk about her."

His father just shrugged.

"A man thing, huh?"

"You got it. Talking is a woman thing." He took another swallow of his beer. "So how did Mrs Newcastle take the news that this Rick Graham really is her son?"

Duncan laid his fork down. *So much for family time,* he thought. "I haven't told her about the second test yet."

"Why?"

"I'm giving Rick some time to accept the situation."

Alex's eyes narrowed. "Rick? Are you involved with this man?"

Duncan swallowed in a suddenly dry throat. "By involved do you mean attracted to, sleeping with, or generally making a fool of myself?"

"All of the above," he snapped.

"I just feel this man's pain. That's all."

"Good grief, you're just like Joan. Get your head on straight. We run an investigating agency and our clients put a lot of trust in us. Mrs Newcastle is our client and *she* is your first priority. Get on that phone and call her this instant."

Duncan slowly stood up, throwing his napkin down onto his plate as he looked at his father. "This is my case and I will handle it my way." He gritted his teeth and counted slowly to three. "A lot of lives will be changed when the DNA results are revealed so I'm taking it slow. If you have a problem with that, you can take me off the payroll."

"Now you listen here..."

Duncan headed for the door. *So much for a nice father-son evening.* Alex had turned into his usual controlling, manipulative... No wonder his mother cried a lot. He felt like crying now.

How could one man make him doubt every decision he'd ever made? He jumped into his car and sat for a moment. Alex wasn't getting to him this time. He'd made the right decision concerning Rick and Mrs Newcastle.

As he backed out of the driveway, he wondered how Duncan was taking the news of the second test. Pulling over to the curb, he pulled out his cell phone and dialled.

No answer.

He either isn't home or he's just not taking calls. Duncan had to talk to him. "Guess that I'm taking another drive to Bowness in the morning."

Chapter Ten

Duncan sighed loudly and took a sip of his rum-and-coke. Rick still wasn't answering his phone.

There was a heavy knock at the door.

"Who can that be at this hour?" It was after midnight. Frowning, Duncan opened it.

Rick stood there, swaying back and forth. He was wearing a plaid shirt and tight black jeans. His *Stetson* was perched crookedly on his head.

"Oh, hi." Duncan swallowed in a suddenly dry throat.

"I thought it was you." Rick was still swaying unsteadily and his words were heavily slurred. "I've seen you prancing about in your undies."

"You have? When?" Duncan frowned at him. *And did you like the show?* He was wearing a grey tee-shirt and boxer shorts right now. He felt his dick twitch. *Down boy.*

"I want to confront my aunt. She's upstairs."

"Okay...about what?"

"You're all trying to ruin my life."

"Come in before you fall down." Duncan grabbed Rick's arm and pulled the other man into his apartment. *Before we give the whole floor a show.* He let the door click closed. "How much have you been drinking?"

"Not enough."

From the brewery smell, Duncan was amazed that Rick was even capable of standing. *He can't drive home like this.*

"She said she saw me born. You say I was kidnapped. The bloody test says I'm not me." Rick blinked his watery eyes repeatedly. "So who the hell am I?"

"You're..." Duncan's voice trailed off. "Good question."

Rick's eyes had closed and he was breathing more heavily.

"Hello?"

Rick's eyelids barely twitched.

"Damn it." Duncan sighed. "Well, you can't sleep standing there in the hallway." He pulled Rick into staggering motion, supporting most of his weight while guiding him down the hallway towards the bedroom. "Pity I just have the one bed."

Moonlight was streaming through the windows.

Duncan stopped by the side of the bed and began to turn Rick around.

Rick collapsed backwards onto the bed.

Taking several deep breaths, Duncan rubbed his arms and stretched out his back. "This wasn't in my job description," he muttered at his drunk guest. "You're the cowboy...steer-wrestling is supposed to be your thing."

Rick made no reply.

Duncan looked down at the sleeping cowboy. "Now what do I do with you?" he muttered. "Hell, I know *exactly* what I want to do with you, but you're too drunk to be much fun." He bit his lip. "On the other hand, you'd never remember any of this happening." Which could have advantages.

"I suppose I'll behave myself." Which sucked, but he was trying to maintain some semblance of a professional relationship. "I can't leave him like this with his feet hanging off the bed."

He bent down to picked up Rick's booted feet and swung his legs around. Now his feet hung off the bed because he wasn't positioned correctly. There wasn't much Duncan could do about that. He stared down at those feet. *He'd probably sleep better without his boots.* How do you remove a cowboy's boots?

Very carefully, he supposed.

With both hands, Duncan grabbed at Rick's right boot and pulled to no avail. Damn. Were they glued on? He placed his foot against the bed for leverage and tried again. He yanked with all his strength. The boot came off so suddenly that he lost his footing and fell backward to the carpet on his ass.

"Damn," he swore. But he did have the boot in his hand.

Still muttering, he got back to his feet and grabbed the other boot. This time, though, he was prepared and maintained his balance. He placed both boots by the closet door. He stared down at the sleeping cowboy.

"I suppose I could take your shirt off for you." His hand went to undo the buttons on Rick's shirt, but as soon as his fingers touched his masculine skin he drew back. "I won't go that far." Rick would not appreciate being stripped by another man. *And I might enjoy it just a bit too much.*

He turned to leave.

Then he turned back. "Fuck it...you owe me this much."

He reached for the front of Rick's shirt and began undoing the buttons. He paused with the shirt half-undone. Yes, very nice." He dropped his hand down to unbuckle Rick's belt, popping the button on his *Levi's* as he did so.

He continued undoing buttons.

"What's this?" As he finished opened the shirt, he could see scarring along Rick's torso. Old burns? They looked serious.

He lifted Rick up slightly so that he could pull Rick's shirt completely off. He hung the shirt on the closet doorknob.

He leaned in close, inhaling the scent of his guest. Rick smelled good. Even with the stale beer on his breath.

"I'm enjoying this, though it'd be a lot more fun if you were conscious too." Duncan unzipped Rick's jeans. He slowly pulled them down the cowboy's muscular legs, savouring every moment, and then tossed them aside.

Rick lay there, on the bed, in just a pair of dark green boxer briefs. The front of his shorts were bulging.

Duncan reached for the bulge—the front of his own boxers were also bulging. "Who are you dreaming about?" he asked softly. He ran his fingers lightly along the other man's crotch. *Oh I want too!* He forced himself to pull his hand away. "I'm not going to cross that line." *But I really really want too!*

Duncan took a step away from the bed and looked down at his guest. "Now I really do wish that I had a larger bed." A queen-sized would be nice...instead of his decades-old twin.

Giving Rick one last regretful look, Duncan picked up a pillow and afghan and walked to the living room and the couch.

* * *

Rick woke up to a pounding drum solo, and eventually realized it was inside his head. *Oh, man.* He clutched his head with both hands. *What the hell was I drinking last night?* Patches of foggy memory began to drift across his aching brain.

After talking to his grandmother, and storming out, he'd stopped in at one of the local bars. The *Boots and Spurs?* Or some other place. He had a beer, then another, and then another. He'd had some whiskey in there, too. The more he drank, the better he felt.

He opened eyes and stared at the ceiling.

"What the hell?" Where was his ceiling fan?

He sat up, then grabbed at his head again.

The sheet slipped down to his waist, baring his skin. He lifted the sheet and looked underneath. He was still wearing his boxer shorts at least. Taking a deep breath, he looked around the room.

He didn't recognize the furnishings, though the room seemed vaguely familiar to him.

"Where the hell am I?" *How much did I drink last night?* He threw the sheet back and stood up. His head was pounding, but he tried to ignore it. *I should've known better than to drink so much.* He spotted his clothes—his jeans were heaped on the floor next to his boots and his shirt was hanging on the door handle of the closet.

"I seem to be alone." He wondered exactly who he had accompanied home. *What did we do last night? Was I am good?* He needed coffee, lots of coffee. As he stood, the room swayed and he sat back down on the edge of the bed again.

What a mess. He hadn't gotten this drunk in a long time.

Before he stopped at whichever bar he'd stopped at, he'd driven around unable to get the DNA test out of his mind. All of his life he'd known exactly who he was—Thomas and Claudia Graham's grandson. Now he wasn't sure.

Doubts mingled with fact and fiction. Who was he?

Light-headed, he stood back up and set out in search of the kitchen. He was desperate for some coffee, but then he realized he had to use the bathroom. The layout of the apartment seemed familiar—it was like his aunt's, though the furnishings were different.

The bathroom was across the hall, just like his aunt's. He washed his hands and then headed towards the kitchen. He stopped to stare into the living room.

A young man lay on his stomach, his short blond hair mussed up against the pillow. Thin cotton boxer shorts moulded what appeared to be a nice tight ass, and an abandoned afghan lay tumbled on the floor. He was sound asleep.

It was Duncan O'Neale.

Rick stared, open-mouthed. "What the hell?" Was this Duncan's apartment then? "What the hell?" he repeated. How had he gotten here? Last night was all a blur to him.

"Did I meet him at the bar and come home with him? Did he take advantage of me?" He doubted it thought. "Where the hell is my truck?" He walked towards the window and looked down into the parking lot. It was definitely the same building his aunt lived in. "I knew that was you I saw that one time." He could see his fire engine red pickup truck. He should leave...get dressed and get the hell out of there before Duncan woke up.

But he knows where I live anyway. I can't hide from him.

The pounding in his head reminded him he had another emergency. Coffee. Coffee first. Then he would leave.

Quickly filling up the kettle and flicking it on, he glanced back at the still-sleeping Duncan. Besides Jennifer Newcastle, he was the last person Rick wanted to see.

* * *

Duncan woke up to the smell of fresh brewed coffee. He stretched and sat up, yawning, but quickly clamped his mouth shut when he saw Rick sitting in a chair, coffee mug in hand, watching him.

"So...about last night." Rick's hair was combed hair and still damp from a shower he'd obviously just finished. He hadn't shaved, but the stubble on his face gave him a sexy rugged look. He was fully dressed, compete with his boots on.

Duncan stood up. "Good morning to you too."

Rick lifted the coffee mug to his mouth. "Good morning."

Duncan walked to the kitchen and poured himself a mug. "Sleep well?"

"Yeah, I guess." Rick followed him. "I kinda helped myself to a few things. The coffee and some aspirin."

"Not a problem." Duncan gave him a grin. "My bed too."

"I wondered where I was when I woke up. So, about last night? It's all rather foggy."

"Given the smell on your breath, I'm not surprised."

"So how did I get here?"

"You drove, God knows how in your condition. You could have killed someone."

Rick flinched.

"You just showed up after midnight. Rattled on about not knowing who you really were. Threatened to go upstairs to your aunt's and have it out with her, but then you passed out in the hallway."

"Oh." Rick looked down at his feet, embarrassed by hearing the events of the previous night. *Was I really that bad?* "But," he lifted his head back up, "I woke up in your bed."

"I couldn't very well leave you in the hallway."

"And you undressed me too?"

"Yep." Duncan gave him a broad smile. "I had to have some fun after all." Then he clamped his mouth closed so fast that his teeth clicked..

Rick narrowed his eyes. "Have some fun?"

Duncan stood silently.

"Does that mean that you're a—"

"Yeah, I'm gay." Duncan threw caution to the wind. "Is that a problem for you, mister macho ex-fireman? Are you all nervous now that you slept in the bed of another man?"

"No, of course not!" Rick heard the defensiveness in his own voice. "It's not the first time. I mean..." He felt his face growing hot.

Duncan stared at him. "Go on."

"I mean, I've slept in other guys' beds before. It's not that big a deal."

"All right then."

Rick was still eying Duncan. *Did you and I do anything last night?* He wanted to ask that question, but he wasn't sure that he really wanted to know the answer.

The silence stretched out somewhat uncomfortably.

"So, why did you go drinking so much last night?" Duncan poured himself a second mug and sat down at the breakfast bar. The kitchen was too small for a table, but there was a nice counter separating the kitchen and living room which made a nice eating nook.

"I got the results of the second test. I went to see my grandmother and aunt. We had a rather heated discussion about my birth and the test."

"Oh."

"Yes. She says it's all ridiculous. She wasn't even angry because it's so absurd."

Duncan shifted uneasily. "But you know something's wrong?"

"Yeah." Rick raised his eyes to meet Duncan's. "You're the private dick. How could this happen?"

Duncan placed his mug onto the counter. "The baby switch would be quite simple to pull off if you both were in the hospital at the same time, but you're the Newcastles checked into the hospital after the Grahams had already left."

"So someone had to go into the hospital and deliberately steal the real baby Rick?"

"Yes."

"So where is the real Rick Graham then?"

Duncan shrugged. "Now *that* is a mystery. I've checked a lot of records from back then and I'm still drawing a blank."

"So my aunt and grandmother are lying or something else is going on."

"Yes. Either way, there's a baby missing." Duncan shook his head. "I want to know the truth...do you?"

Rick nodded his head. "Yeah, I do."

* * *

Rick sat in his truck. He looked up towards the apartment building. He forced his eyes away from Duncan's windows to the floor above.

He hadn't been up to see his aunt, and now he wasn't sure that he wanted to go and confront her a second time.

Duncan had left for work—after having told Rick to call him later if he wanted to talk or anything.

"I'm not ready to see her," he told himself. Maybe it was being cowardly, but maybe Pamela was right and dragging the DNA test results into the open would be a mistake.

"I don't know what to do," he muttered. It was a new feeling for him.

Rick started the truck's ignition.

Chapter Eleven

Duncan nodded his head, trying to maintain a neutral expression on his face. "Of course I'm sure of everything I've told you," he told the man sitting across from him.

Mario Iorillo was glaring.

"I've been able to take plenty of pictures." He handed over the file. His camera skills had never been perfect—he certainly wouldn't win any journalism awards—but Danielle's face was clearly recognizable as she climbed out of her car and entered the motel.

Mario let the papers fall onto the desktop. "I was hoping that I was wrong," he said in his accented voice. "I really thought I was wrong."

"I wish you had been too," Duncan told him. "I'm sorry."

"Do you know how the other man is?"

"Well, that is the interesting part of this. I lingered in the parking lot a few times after your wife had left...and I did get a picture or two." He handed them over.

Mario stared at the brunette in wide-eyed amazement.

"She signs the registry as Juliette Wilson," Duncan told his client. "She's apparently a travelling saleswoman who always stays overnight on her way to and from her various businesses. She checks out after your wife leaves."

Mario shook his head. "My wife is having an affair with another *woman*?"

"Your wife is *meeting* another woman," Duncan pointed out. "They might just be old friends getting together to talk."

"Do you really believe that?"

"No, I don't."

"Neither do I." Mario dropped the photos back onto the desk.

Duncan wasn't sure what to say.

"Thank you for your services, Mister O'Neale." Mario rose to his feet. "I believe we're done." He gathered up the photos and Duncan's typed report. "I'll pay the final instalment of your bill before I leave."

Duncan nodded his head. "Of course. Is there anything I else I can do for you?"

"No...I think this matter is now between my wife and myself."

Duncan winced at his harsh tone. "Think of your children," he said. "Before you confront her and say or do anything unforgivable."

Mario looked startled by his words.

"You might be able to work this out."

"Thank you for the advice," Mario told him. "I'll think about it."

Duncan carefully filed Mario's cheque, taking a moment to rapidly glance through the other invoices and account statements. *I'll have to take care of this paperwork soon,* he thought.

The door to his father's office opened.

Duncan looked up.

"Well?" Alex asked him.

"Well?" Duncan asked back.

"Have you cleaned up that Newcastle case yet?"

"I have it under control."

"Do you, boy?"

"Yes."

"Then you're done wasting time? There are other cases to be looked after."

"I just cleaned up two of them. Mario Iorillo has paid in full. And I was talking to on the phone with Violet Sherwood and she's finally accepted that her husband is *not* having an affair. Apparently he's been working all this extra overtime so that he could afford to take her on a Caribbean cruise."

"So it's one happy ending at least. That should make you happy, mister dreamer. Always chasing the fairy tale *happily ever after*."

Duncan nodded.

Alex grunted. "Don't get involved," he said. "That's the key to being a successful investigator. Trust no one. Dig for all of the facts. Don't get emotionally involved."

"That's easy for you to say," Duncan told him. "You never want to show your emotions to anyone. The rest of us human beings don't have that ability."

Alex snorted.

"Anyway, I'm thinking about taking the next couple of days off."

"Oh?" Alex's eyes narrowed.

"Yeah." Rick looked his father squarely in the eyes. "There's nothing around here that's pressing right now and I need some personal time."

"Going away? Where?"

"It's personal."

"Mmm." Alex took a step towards him. "Duncan Graham." His mouth twisted around the name.

"Maybe. Maybe not. Anyway, it's my business."

"Boy..."

"See you later, Dad." Duncan hurried back to his office and closed the door with a firm *thump*. It might be cowardly, but he didn't want to hear any more from Alex regarding his opinion of Duncan.

If he only knew that Duncan spent last night in my bed, he thought. *And if only* I'd *spent the night in* my *bed!* He closed his eyes and thought back to the thrill he'd experienced while stripping the ex-fireman. His hand drifted down to the front of his jeans.

"I suppose I could take your shirt off for you." Duncan's hand went to undo the buttons on Rick's shirt, but as soon as his fingers touched his masculine skin he drew back. "I won't go that far." Rick would not appreciate being stripped by another man. *And I might enjoy it just a bit too much.*

He turned to leave.

Then he turned back. "Fuck it...you owe me this much."

He reached for the front of Rick's shirt and began undoing the buttons. He paused with the shirt half-undone. Yes, very nice." He dropped his hand down to unbuckle Rick's belt, popping the button on his *Levi's* as he did so.

He continued undoing buttons.

"What's this?" As he finished opened the shirt, he could see scarring along Rick's torso. Old burns? They looked serious.

He lifted Rick up slightly so that he could pull Rick's shirt completely off. He hung the shirt on the closet doorknob.

He leaned in close, inhaling the scent of his guest. Rick smelled good. Even with the stale beer on his breath.

"I'm enjoying this, though it'd be a lot more fun if you were conscious too." Duncan unzipped Rick's jeans. He slowly pulled them down the cowboy's muscular legs, savouring every moment, and then tossed them aside.

Rick lay there, on the bed, in just a pair of dark green boxer briefs. The front of his shorts were bulging.

Duncan reached for the bulge—the front of his own boxers were also bulging. "Who are you dreaming about?" he asked softly. He ran his fingers lightly along the other man's crotch. *Oh I want too!* He forced himself to pull his hand away. "I'm not going to cross that line." *But I really really want too!*

And then Duncan carefully pulled opened Rick's fly.

The hard-on popped out.

Duncan licked his lips.

Rick was snoring softly.

Duncan bent down and took the hard shaft into his mouth. Rick moaned softly, but he was sleeping as only a passed-out drunk could. He was really hard and Duncan was enjoying himself immensely.

He sucked the ex-fireman off, teasing him shaft with his tongue. Rick moaned and shifted his legs slightly. Duncan kept sucking him until finally he gave a twitch and began to shoot out his load.

The phone rang.

"Hello, O'Neale Investigations." Duncan managed to sound mostly businesslike, even if slightly distracted. He tried stuffing his throbbing hard-on back into his jeans with just his left hand.

"*Hi, Duncan. It's Rick Graham.*"

"Oh hi, Rick. What's up?"

"*I was thinking about you.*"

So was I, Duncan thought as he continued to try and pull himself back together. *Go down, you stupid thing!* The more he struggled with his dick, the harder he was getting.

"*Can you stop by the farm later?*"

"Of course, I can."

"*I want to talk to you about...things.*" Rick laughed, somewhat bitterly. "*I need to talk to someone and you're the only one I can think of.*"

"I'll be there this afternoon," Duncan told him.

"*Thanks, Duncan.*"

"Anytime."

"*Listen, why don't you stay for supper? I've been hankering after a decent barbequed burger. Just as easy to grill for two as one.*"

"Now that sounds like a great idea. I'll bring some salads."

"*You don't have to do that.*"

"No, but I want too.

"*All right. See you later.*"

Duncan hung up the phone, then he looked down at himself. "I need to get my act together." He had it bad for the cowboy. *Real bad.*

Chapter Twelve

"Oh shit!"

Duncan stared at the video on the television screen.

Rick's face was flushed and he was still struggling to zip his jeans back up. "I didn't hear you come in."

"I gathered that you were...preoccupied." Duncan looked back at the video and his mouth twitched into a grin. "The one on the left is quite a hunk."

Rick licked his lips nervously. "I didn't plan for this to happen," he said. "For you to walk in on me like this." He reached the remote and the screen went blank.

"You don't have to turn it off on my account." Duncan sat down on the leather couch. "I might enjoy seeing it."

Rick was still flushed. "It's just, that is, I'm not used too—"

"I know. You're the macho guy." Duncan chuckled at him. "So, you're gay. That's not much of a shock these days."

"I know," Rick replied, "but it still takes some getting used too. For some people it is a big deal."

"Your secret is safe with me." Duncan paused. He looked at the bulge in the other man's jeans, and thought about the quick glimpse that he'd managed to get of his cock.

"Thanks." Rick slumped back into his chair. "I've gotten used to hiding it. The guys at the fire station wouldn't have been happy sharing the showers with a cocksucker."

"So much for that fantasy," Duncan commented.

Rick stared at him for a moment, then he burst out laughing.

"I was glad that you called. I came here today to discuss your other secret. You have a sister who is very eager to finally meet you."

"But I don't want to meet her." Rick shook his head. "I don't want to be this Jefferson Newcastle. It sounds so pretentious."

"So, be someone else. You've been you for how many decades now?"

Rick rose to his feet. The front of his jeans were still bulging. "Do you want to go for a ride?" he asked abruptly.

Duncan frowned.

"Horseback I mean. It always helps me think. With a saddle if you can't handle barebacking." Rick managed a weak grin. "Or are you a purebred city-boy?"

"I can ride." Duncan stood up and took a step forward. "Saddle me up a horse and I'll show you how well I can ride a proper mount."

* * *

After a quick drink, Rick led Duncan to the barn. "Put this on, city-boy." He tossed Duncan a hat. "The sun will burn you to a crisp." It was a cloudy day, so the heat wasn't bad, but the sun would be scorching if the weather cleared up.

Duncan pulled the hat onto his head. He felt more like a cowboy now, though in sneakers instead of boots.

Rick led two horses out of their stalls. "This is Morning Mist. She's a gentle mare."

"Oh." Duncan stroked the horse's face. "You think I need gentle?"

"Yep," Rick nodded his head. "Until I know how you can ride." He swung a saddle onto Star's back. "Tighten up the saddle with these straps."

Duncan did as he was told.

Rick watched him, then saddled his own horse. "Let's ride, city-boy."

Duncan hadn't been in the saddle for a while, but he adjusted quickly. "Like riding a bike," he said. "Once you learn, you never really forget."

The ranch covered many acres. The land was very. Some pastures had been cleared to make hay fields. Others had towering trees with grass growing lushly beneath them. Red-faced cattle grazed contentedly.

"What kind of cattle are those?" Duncan asked as they rode through a herd.

"Hereford."

The barbed wire fence stretched past the horizon. The sun was currently behind a cloud, so it wasn't overwhelmingly hot just then.

"You ride pretty well...for a city-boy."

Duncan laughed at the comment. "I'm a bit out of practice."

Rick reined in his horse. He pulled off his *Stetson* and fanned his face with it. "I'd almost swear you'd been riding before I met you."

"Maybe I did." Duncan chuckled, though he kept a tight grip on the reins. "Dad arranged for me to take lessons years ago...but like I said earlier, it's just like riding a bike. You don't forget the lessons." He sighed. "Or the old bruises."

"Bruises?"

"Well, my riding lessons ended after I fell off the horse for the fifth time. Mom overreacted when she was called to the hospital. It was just a broken arm...it healed."

Rick shook his head. "Lucky you."

They rode along the fence line.

"How far does this go?"

"A long, long way." Rick waved his hand. "Got to have it to keep the cattle from straying."

"You have cattle?"

"Yes and no. I have some cattle, but they're actually Jerry's. I just rent him the pastures to use."

"Oh."

Rick licked his lips. "Thanks, Duncan."

"For what?"

"For trying to help me out with everything."

"It's okay, cowboy." Duncan wiped his hand across his face. "Maybe one day you'll let me drive your big old truck."

"No way, city-boy." Rick shook his head. "It only responds to me."

"Like your horse?"

"You bet."

"Cowboys sure have odd habits."

"City-boy, if you only knew."

Duncan felt himself smile. The way Rick said city-boy made him feel and warm and gooey inside. His heart raced a bit faster and he realized just how strong his feeling for the other man really were getting. But do you feel the same way about me? he wondered.

They rode in silence for a bit longer.

"There's a nice creek just a bit further," Rick announced. "Meanders its way through several properties out here."

"I bet it's a nice to cool off in after a long ride." Duncan could feel the sweat trickling down his back.

"Oh, it is." Rick chuckled. "I've gone skinny dipping there so many times."

Duncan's ears perked up at that. "That the creek that developer wanted to divert?"

"Yeah, but he lost the case." Rick pointed. "There it is." He dug through one of his saddlebags.

Duncan looked. He could see the thicker, green grass which grew on the banks. "Doesn't look all the big from here."

"It is." Rick took a drink from a canteen, then handed it to Duncan. "Drink some."

"What is it?"

"Water. You don't want to get dehydrated out here in the heat. And I have peanut butter crackers."

"I love a man who's prepared." Duncan took a swig from the canteen.

"I'm always prepared."

"Good to know." Duncan gave him back the canteen.

"It's important to be ready for anything. Especially in winter...you never know what the weather is gonna throw at you."

Duncan stared at the creek. "It looks really nice and inviting." He dismounted from Morning Mist with a groan. "I need a minute." He collapsed into the grass. "I can't ride any longer."

"You lasted longer than I thought you would," Rick told him. He squatted down and began to remove Duncan's sneakers.

He frowned. "What..."

"The creek water is cool. It'll rejuvenate you."

"That might take more than cool water."

Rick effortlessly slipped off his own boots and then removed his socks. Rolling up his jeans, he gave Duncan a smile. "Come on."

Duncan quickly finished removing his shoes and socks. The ground was hard and dry beneath his feet, but the water was cool. Even the mud squishing between his toes felt wonderful. "Oh, this is great," he exclaimed. "I want to submerge my whole body."

"Go ahead. The water is deeper over here."

Duncan looked up, startled by the suggestion. It was still afternoon, but the place was in the middle of nowhere. "What the hell." He waded back to shore and quickly removed his tee-shirt and jeans, throwing them onto the bank.

Rick did the same. He stood there, in his boxer briefs, for just a moment, and then slid them down his legs.

Duncan stared.

"What you looking at, city-boy?" Rick did not bother to try and cover himself with his hands.

"Just enjoying the view." Duncan shucked off his own boxers. He had a semi, but that fact didn't matter to him.

Rick dunked himself into the water and Duncan hastily did the same. Together they sank beneath the cool surface.

Duncan eyed the other man.

Rick was floating in the water, looking completely relaxed.

Duncan could feel his dick growing harder. *Should I?* he wondered. Rick eyed him, seemingly at ease. Duncan sighed. *I guess not.* Hidden by the water, he started to stroke himself...and wonder if Rick was watching him through those apparently closed eyes.

"I'm getting hungry." Standing by his horse, Rick adjusted his hat and bent to check the saddle straps. "We should head back to the house."

"Sounds like a plan." Duncan finished tying his shoes. He hadn't managed to get himself off while relaxing in the water, though his erection had eventually gone away.

"So...do you have a boyfriend?"

Are you offering? Duncan shook his head. "Nope, I'm single."

"I was just curious...didn't want to cause any trouble for you. I mean, you seem to spend so much time here lately."

"No worries about that. I live alone—you saw that—so I doubt anyone has even noticed how much I'm away."

"Good." Rick licked his lips. "I mean that you're not going to have been missed I mean. Wouldn't want half the cops in Calgary out looking for you."

"There's no fear of that."

Chapter Thirteen

The sun was setting and the sky was as spectacular as only an Albertan sky could be. A cool breeze was blowing, making the back deck the most comfortable place to be.

Duncan stared towards the Rocky Mountains. "That sky is amazing." He took a sip from his beer.

"One of the best things about being out of the city," Rick agreed. "The dawn sunrise is just as amazing."

"I'll have to try and see one of those sometime."

"Yeah," Rick replied after a long silence.

Duncan licked his lips. *Wrong thing to say?* He chuckled softly, trying to lighten the mood. "I'm getting hungry...how about you?"

"Yeah, I am."

Duncan pulled open the door and stepped inside the kitchen. He held the door for Rick to follow him in. "I bet your view of the stars is amazing too."

"Yep. On a clear night, you can lose yourself in the universe."

"That sounds poetic."

"I'm a man of many talents." Rick belched loudly. "See?" he asked, laughing just as loudly.

Duncan and set his empty beer bottle down by the sink. "We should put those burgers on." He pulled a fresh, cold bottle from the fridge. "You want another?"

"Sounds like a plan." Rick brushed his hand through his black hair. "I've left my hat out in the barn."

"I'll get it for you. You can get the burgers out." Duncan set his beer down on the counter. "I'll be right back." He stepped outside.

"This is gonna be good." Rick opened the fridge and pulled out the tray of beef patties he'd made up earlier that morning. The macaroni and potato salads also looked amazing. Duncan had claimed that the macaroni seasoning was a family secret, and he grinned as his stomach rumbled. "This is gonna be real good."

Balancing the tray in his hand, he pushed open the door and stepped out onto the step. "Duncan, what did you want to put on—shit!"

The barn was burning brightly.

Rick dropped the plate and leaped off the deck.

"Duncan?" Rick called out.

The barn door was swinging open and two horses were galloping across the pasture. No mistaking Thunderhead and Misty Morning.

"Duncan?"

Thick smoke was billowing into the sky.

"Duncan?" Rick peered through the smoke, trying to see movement within the barn. There were flames everywhere and the heat was scorching on his face. "Duncan?" He started through the door, but a hand grabbed his arm and hauled him backwards.

"Shit, Rick, you can't go in there."

Rick continued struggling. "Let go of me!"

Jerry shook his head and kept pulling him back. "No way. It's a lost-cause now."

"But I think Duncan's in there."

Jerry let go of his arm in shock. "What?"

"Duncan!" Rick plunged through the doorway.

Rick's eyes were watering fiercely and he could barely breath in the smoke. Coughing, he stooped low to the floor, trying to pull in enough clean air to call out.

Knots in the old wooden beams crackled and popped loudly.

"Duncan!"

As the smoke eddied, he spotted an arm peaking through the open gate on one of the stalls.

Rick dragged Duncan into the cool night air.

Jerry threw a bucket of water onto them both and Rick gasped at the sudden cold shock.

Duncan opened his eyes and coughed. "I think I got all the horses out," he wheazed.

"You damn fool! What the hell were you doing in there?"

"I went to get your hat." Duncan coughed again. "I lost it."

"Who cares about the damned hat? You could've been killed."

Jerry nodded, his face pale in the firelight. "That was too close." He was already refilling the bucket from the trough. "We're not gonna be able to save it."

Rick wasn't listening to him.

* * *

Duncan stepped out through the hospital doors. His face was cleaned up, but his clothes still stank of wood smoke.

"You're okay?"

"A little smelly and tired, but otherwise good. How're the horses?"

"They're spooked, but otherwise fine." Rick was openly surprised by the question. *I wouldn't have expected a city-boy to ask about them.* "Jerry is looking after them for me."

"And did you save the barn?"

"Nope."

"Damn."

"It can be rebuilt." Rick coughed. There were still sooty streaks on his shirt and face. "You're the one I'm worried about."

"I'll fine after a good night's sleep." Duncan managed to give a convincing smile. "If I wasn't, would they have let me go home?"

"Your father is gonna kill us both, you do realize that."

"Yeah, probably."

"My truck is over there." Rick hooked his thumb towards it.

"Like I can miss it." Duncan chuckled. "That colour stands out in any parking lot."

"I like it." He followed after Duncan, watching the other man closely. "So what the hell happened? How did the barn catch on fire?"

Duncan shrugged. "It's a mystery. I went into the barn to get your hat," he told Rick. "The door was closed, but it wasn't locked. I went to Thunderhead's stall to get your hat and then..."

"And then?"

"I thought I saw something move, in the back."

"There was always too much junk in there." Rick kicked at a clod of dirt with the toe of his boot.

"I went to check it out." Duncan shrugged. "Old habits, I guess. Anyway, I got close but saw nothing. Figured it was just my imagination. When I turned around, the doors were swinging closed and then the flames were everywhere."

"Damn."

"I want to make sure the horses were free—they were both rearing and screaming. When I pulled the latch on Thunderhead's stall, he clipped me with his hoof and knock me flat.

"The next thing I know, is you hauling me out of there."

* * *

The barn was still-smouldering ash, with a few charred beams standing forlornly amid the rubble.

"It's gone." Duncan blinked his eyes feeling tears well up at Rick's loss.

"It can be rebuilt later. It's just an old barn." Rick cleared his throat. "The horses are staying at Jerry's. They're fine." He had just seen his friend off—Jerry had stayed at the farm while Rick had rushed to the hospital.

"Oh." Duncan walked towards the rubble, studying it. "It was deliberately set...had to have been."

Privately, Rick agreed. "But who the hell would've set it?"

"You got any enemies?"

"I've sparked some arguments with people, but who hasn't? I didn't think I'd crossed anyone bad enough for this though."

"Not even that developer?"

Rick shook his head. "I cost him some land for a new condo. He's since built up near that new mall and is raking in a fortune. Losing to me was probably the best thing that could've happened to him."

"Yeah, but still. Your barn is gone. Shit."

"And you nearly got yourself killed! Don't do it again."

Duncan smiled. "You were worried?"

"What? No...it's just that I had to go in there after you and *I* could've been killed."

"Oh."

"Yeah, oh." Rick kicked at a clod of dirt. "Anyway, you need some sleep and so do I."

"But what about the—"

"Jerry had the volunteer fire brigade in. He looked after everything."

"I don't recall it."

"You were in the ambulance by then." He stared at the wreckage. "I followed along afterwards. After I'd had a chance to settle my nerves."

"Oh."

"I'll have the inspectors out later to investigate."

Duncan yawned so widely, that his jaw cracked.

"We need to get you to bed."

Duncan shook his head. "My keys are on your counter."

Rick shook his head. "You're not driving back to Calgary. Not in your condition. Come on inside with me."

Duncan let himself be led back towards the house.

They stepped inside the kitchen.

"Let me help you with those." Rick knelt down to pull off Duncan's sneakers. "Man, you reek."

"You don't smell that great yourself," Duncan replied. He yawned and rubbed tiredly at his eyes. "Just let me curl up on the couch for an hour or two…I'll be fine."

"No, you're sleeping in my bed."

Duncan blinked.

"I'll sleep on the couch."

"Oh." Duncan could hear the disappointment plain in his voice. He gave his head a shake. "I mean, I don't want to put you out."

"You're not." Rick cleared his throat. "I owe you for a night already."

Duncan grinned at him.

"But right now, you need a shower. Hell, we both do." Rick gestured towards the bathroom. "Move it." Rick paused, noting the blinking light on the answering machine. "I'll let you get started while I check my messages. My granny's been ill and I don't want to—"

"Go ahead." Duncan nodded. "I'll be fine."

Rick was just unbuttoning his shirt as he stepped into the bathroom. "Haven't you gotten the shower running?"

"I'm working on it." Duncan had taken his shirt off and his jeans were unzipped. He was swaying slightly. "Anything important?"

"No." Rick narrowed his eyes. "You gonna be okay in there?"

"Yeah, of course." Duncan nodded. "But I won't object if you want to join me."

Rick laughed. "All right." He dropped his shirt into the hamper, and followed it with his jeans. His boxers bulged, the material straining across his crotch. "Let me help you with those." He steadied Duncan, while pulling down his dirty jeans.

Duncan's own boxers were bulging.

"What's got you all excited?" Rick asked.

"Being near you," Duncan replied honestly. "You are fucking hot."

Rick smiled and yanked down the private eye's boxers.

The shower was running warm and refreshing.

> The two men soaped and rinsed each other at a leisurely pace under the steamy spray, washing away the stench of wood smoke.

Duncan half-hoped this joint-shower might finally lead to a bout of sex, but he had to admit that he really didn't feel up to it. *I can't do my fantasies justice,* he thought. His hard-on wasn't going away though.

Rick smiled at him, the soapy water washing over and temporarily smoothing down the hair covering his head and body. "Now it's your turn," he said as he reach out.

Duncan let himself be pulled closer to the other man.

Their bodies trembled as they kissed feverishly, rubbing up against each other. Rick was also sporting a hard-on and Duncan lovingly tugged on it.

Rick laughed. "You sure know how to handle it, city-boy."

"You're the ex-fireman…you could probably give me some pointers on handling my hose." He continued stroking the other man's erection.

"You are incredible."

"So are you." Duncan was in ecstasy as Rick stroked the back of his neck, before caressing his erect nipples and sucking on them.

"You need your sleep," Rick finally announced. "Come on." He turned the water off.

Duncan groaned, reluctant to see their fun coming to an end. "That felt really nice."

"Yeah, but you some sleep."

Rick stepped out of the shower and grabbed a fluffy towel from the rack. "Here, let me help you."

After they were both dried, Rick led Duncan into the bedroom. "Lay down." He pulled the blankets down.

Duncan collapsed into the bed. "Oh," he moaned as he stretched out. "This feels so good."

Rick climbed into bed next to him. "I'm glad you're all right."

"I'm glad I saved your horses." Duncan yawned, his jaw cracking. "Sorry."

"It's okay." Rick smiled at him.

Duncan laid his head against Rick's chest. "I like that look of challenge in your eyes," he mumbled sleepily. "Loved it from the photos too." He thought he said that last part, but he was asleep before Rick could reply.

Chapter Fourteen

"I've got nothing clean to wear."

Rick yawned and twisted his head around to look at the man laying in bed next to him. "You can borrow something of mine until I wash the laundry."

"I can wear my stuff home and wash it there."

"No point in that. I gotta run a load of my own anyway."

"Are you sure?"

"Yeah. What's your rush to get away?"

"Oh, no rush." Duncan stretched out, then snuggled back up against Rick's body. "No rush at all."

Rick rolled out of bed. He stood there, for a moment, then pulled the curtains open.

Duncan stared. "You look amazing right now." He eyed the healed-up burns on Rick's back and legs.

The afternoon sunlight was bathing Rick's torso and arms in a rich golden glow.

> "Another benefit to country living is the lack of next-door neighbours," Rick told him. "I can walk around naked as much as I want."

> "I like the sound of that."

> "How would you like it if I did this?" Rick returned to the bed. He slid in and pulled Duncan roughly to him. "Followed by this?" He pressed his lips hard against the other man's, probing deeply with his tongue.

"Mmm." Rick's five o'clock shadow was like sandpaper against Duncan's face, but he didn't complain. He loved the way it felt. Duncan also loved the feeling of Rick's hard-on pressing against his thigh. Of course, his own cock was throbbing as well.

Rick kissed his way down his chest, following the trail of soft hair, right down the centre. He stopped long enough to flick his tongue in Duncan's navel for a moment, and then continued working his way lower down his body.

"I've been waiting for this moment," Duncan moaned.

"So have I...I wanted to jump you in the creek. Watching you playing with yourself like that."

"So why didn't you?"

"I didn't pack any condoms."

"Oh."

Rick gave him a grin. "Come over here and sit on my chest," he ordered.

Duncan quickly straddled the tight six-pack abs and rubbed his balls on the other man's chest hair. Pre-cum was already pouring out of Rick's dick and it made a nicely lubed surface on which Duncan could glide.

"Lean back, just a little," Rick told him. His cock was getting wetter, and he began to rub it slowly along the crack of Duncan's ass.

Duncan knew what was going to happen—finally! "Oh yeah," he said.

"Good."

Duncan bent down, still straddling Rick's chest, and sucked on his nipples. He bit them ever so softly and reached behind to rub his balls. Rick's cock was still in the crack of his ass, and he could feel the juices slowly lubing his tight hole. "Do it," he begged.

Rick reached for the nightstand and pulled out a foil package. He tore it open and quickly unrolled the condom, sliding it over his shaft. He squirted lube onto the end.

Duncan repositioned himself on top of his new lover. He bent down to kiss Rick. As he broke the kiss and leaned back, he could feel the cold lube rubbing his hole. "Do it," he repeated.

With one quick thrust, Rick pushed inside.

Duncan gasped at the sudden pain. His back went rigid and his entire body trembled. For a moment, the feeling was so intense that he felt as if he might faint.

"Relax," Rick soothed. "I'll go slow."

Duncan nodded.

Rick grabbed his ass cheeks and pulled them further apart, at the same time lifting Duncan up just a little, so he could get a little more room to pump.

It had been too long since Duncan had felt anything this good. His own cock was still rock hard, leaking pre-cum. Rick kept thrusting and Duncan gasped as he enjoyed the sensations.

Rick's teeth were bared into a fierce grin, as if he was the one riding a galloping steed. His thrusts quickened and deepened and Duncan felt himself swaying in time.

Rick plunged himself deeper and deeper, his breathing grew shallow, and his face started to turn red.

Duncan couldn't hold back anymore and cried out as he shot what felt like an endless stream across Rick's chest and face. It just kept coming. Load after load.

Rick grunted loudly and bucked his hips. "Fuck yeah!"

Duncan groaned, sitting there with Rick still inside him.

Slowly, he lifted himself off the other man.

Rick looked at him, gobs of white goo on his stubble. "Wow." He reached up to Duncan's face and gently caressed his cheek. "That's all I can say...just wow."

Duncan slumped down beside him. "*Wow* is right." He gently dragged his fingers along Rick's chest, smearing his cum through the chest hairs and along the old scars. "I feel like a champion bull rider."

"Isn't that my job?"

"I'm a quick learner."

"Well, I'll have to see what other tricks I can teach you." Rick stretched out his arms and groaned. "I need to go and clean up."

"You do that...I need more sleep."

Rick stepped out of the bathroom—the washer was already chugging—and returned to the bedroom. "Hey, city-boy, what can I get you?" he asked.

Duncan kept his arm covering his eyes. "Another six hours of sleep," he mumbled.

Rick chuckled. "That would be nice, but we should get up. I've got to go and check on my horses."

"Damn, that's right." Duncan threw back the covers.

"Damn is right." Rick whistled.

Duncan felt his cheek flush. "It's a perfectly normal reaction," he announced.

"Of course it is."

Duncan stumbled into the bathroom.

"You can use my comb," Rick called out. "You already know where it is." He pulled open a drawer in his dresser and took out a fresh pair of boxer shorts.

* * *

They were sipping their coffee out on the front veranda, when Jerry pulled up in his truck. He climbed out and gave them a friendly wave. "Afternoon, Rick. How are you feeling, Duncan?"

"I'm fine. Thanks for asking."

"Good." Jerry coughed. He stuffed his hands into the back pockets of his worn jeans. "I'm glad you're okay. That was quite the fire last night." He looked over at the burned out barn.

Duncan chuckled. "I like barbeques as much as the next guy, but not when I'm the main course."

Jerry winced.

"So how're the horses?"

"Still restless. I'm letting them run the pasture."

"Good." Rick nodded. "Duncan let them out of their stalls before the smoke got too thick."

"Smart thinking, but you shouldn't have gone into that fire."

"The barn wasn't on fire when I went in."

Jerry winced.

"Must have been an accident. Maybe a wire sparked." Rick shrugged. "I'm just glad that you're alive and well."

Jerry nodded his head. "Yeah, it's a miracle."

"It's a mystery." Duncan took a deep breath. "The barn and your birth, both of them are. Well, I'm a private dick, right?"

"Yeah," Rick agreed.

"Well, then this is my chance to be *your* private dick. What, that didn't come out right."

"It sounded just right to me," Rick told him.

Chapter Fifteen

Duncan walked through the empty hallway. Even down in the basement, the place smelled like a hospital. Antiseptic.

A hospital orderly was leading him and muttering his head slowly. "I'm still not sure about letting you do this."

Duncan patted the other man on his shoulder. "Harry, I'm not looking for anything confidential. The information I want is practically public domain."

"I still don't—"

"I'll owe you a really big favour."

"I could lose my job over this."

"Who will ever know? I promise you, your name will never come up. It's a personal investigation, not a public one."

"I hope so." Harry opened a door and led Duncan into one of the storerooms. "The files here are so old they're still mostly on paper." He gestured towards the rows of large metal filing cabinets. "We'd begun transferring them to the computer, but the staff funding was cut way back."

"I see." Duncan exhaled sharply. "At least tell that these are alphabetized or something."

"Of course they are." Harry nodded his head. "What are we looking for?"

"*We?*"

"I'm not leaving you down here on your own. If you get caught down here, I'll be in deep shit. No point in making it worse." He waited.

"I need the records on two patients. Jefferson Newcastle and Richard Graham." He reeled off the dates of birth from memory.

Harry opened one of the filing cabinets and shuffled through the folders. "You said Jefferson Newcastle?"

"Yeah."

"Well, let's see...ah, here it is."

Duncan took the folder and read through its contents. "Short and to the point." He shook his head and handed the folder back. "Just like what the public record says."

"So you already know this? Then why come here?" Harry asked.

"I wanted to see the original records. Just in case there was some detail I had missed."

"Oh." Harry put the Newcastle folder back and then moved to another cabinet. "Richard Graham." He pulled out the file.

Duncan read it. His eyes narrowed in shock. "This can't be right," he exclaimed.

"What can't be right?"

"This folder." Duncan almost dropped the papers. "This might explain a lot though."

* * *

Pamela looked across the table at him. "And what can I do for you, Mister O'Neale."

Duncan gave her one of his professional smiles. He had been surprised by how easily she agreed to this meeting. "I'm doing a little investigating for Rick."

"Oh?"

"Both of the DNA tests came back as positive matches that he is not a Graham...but a Newcastle."

"And your point is?"

"What can you tell me about the car wreck?"

Pamela shook her head. "I'm not sure what you're getting at."

"Rick's parents were killed when they car was sideswiped by a tractor trailer. They were killed outright. Their baby son was taken to the hospital...with serious injuries." Duncan stared at her. "He died the next day."

Silently, Pamela shook her head.

"Rick's grandparents were out of town, but the hospital records say that *you* identified the bodies of Sarah and Michael Graham. You were there."

"I think that you stole a baby boy from the hospital nursery and passed him off as your nephew."

Pamela stared at him, her mouth hanging open.

"What do you think about my theory?" He waited for her answer.

* * *

"This is gonna taste so good." Rick popped the cap off a bottle and took a long swallow. "I need it to wash the taste of this whole thing out of my mouth." He looked across the room.

Duncan was standing in the doorway to the living room. "I'm not sure what else to tell you. The facts are there." He was having trouble believing them himself.

Rick shook his head. "I can't believe it."

There was a knock on the door.

"It's open so come on in!" he called out. "Aunt Pam."

Pamela was dressed in a long black dress, with a wide-brimmed hat atop her head.

Rick frowned at her. "You look like you're in mourning."

"I am." She licked her lips nervously. "I have to make a confession, Rickie. Something I'm not proud of. A secret I wish had remained buried." Her eyes flicked towards Duncan.

Rick's face had gone pale under his tan.

"We were so happy when Sarah gave birth to her son. Claudia and Thomas were overjoyed and had made plans to cut short their stay in the Maritimes. They were due to fly in on the ninth, but a late spring storm delayed their plane.

"Michael picked his wife and son from the hospital and drove them home...meeting with a truck."

Rick collapsed into one of the kitchen chairs.

Duncan let the silence drag out for a long time, nervously licking his lips. He didn't want to ask the question, but he could see that Rick was unable too. "What happened next?"

"I got the phone call from the hospital. It was like a nightmare. The accident, the injuries to the baby...I don't even remember driving there. I couldn't call Claudia. I knew there had to have been some mistake. It was some other car. Some other Michael and Sarah.

"But it was them. The morgue was cold and they had only been cleaned up a bit. Just enough to make their faces recognizable.

"And then the baby died." Pamela's voice was devoid of emotion as she recited her story.

"In just one night, our family had lost everything. I was numb...and I knew that the shock would kill Claudia."

Duncan had closed his eyes.

Rick stared emptily at the tabletop.

Pamela took a deep breath. "I was on the verge of a breakdown. I just wandered the hospital. It was the middle of the night. The whole place was in semidarkness...no one was in the halls. I reached the nursery floor, not even realizing where I was, and I wandered through it. There was only one nurse on duty, but she didn't seem to see me. I stared through the windows at the sleeping babies.

"It wasn't fair. Such a healthy baby stolen away from us before he'd ever had a chance to live.

"And then I saw you."

Rick flinched.

"I slipped into the room. I saw your black hair and I picked you up in my arms. You stretched and opened your eyes. They were blue and I knew that the hospital had made a mistake. Rick Graham had not died...some other baby had died. You were alive and healthy.

"I grabbed a blanket and wrapped you up in it. I hurried out of the hospital."

"And no one saw you?"

"No." Pamela shook her head. "No one."

Rick was shaking his head. "I don't believe this."

"I took you home with me and then I called Claudia and Thomas. They were still snowed in, waiting for a new flight. I had to break the news about Michael and Sarah, but I told them that you were all right. The shock was too much and Claudia had a mild heart attack.

"I could barely stand the strain of that. I made arrangements for Michael and Sarah's cremations...and their baby. All to share one urn, as per their own request. Then I caught the next plane to Nova Scotia to be with my parents.

"I left Brandon to deal with the paperwork and arrangements. We had been having a few arguments, but I knew he would do that much for me. He knew that I had to go to my mother's bedside."

"And you took the baby with you?"

"Yes, of course. I believe that seeing you was the only thing to keep Claudia alive."

Rick had squeezed his eyes closed. The just-opened beer bottle was forgotten.

"Claudia recovered." Duncan's voice was not a question. "And they never questioned you?"

"No...they never knew the truth. Brandon had everything dealt with before we came back to Calgary. By then, Claudia and Thomas had taken you to raise as their grandson."

"Why—" Rick's voice broke. "Why didn't you keep me?"

"I couldn't face you day after day. Part of me was consumed with guilt at what I had done, but I couldn't take you back. It would have killed Mom for certain. I took up drinking too much and having nightmares and picking fights with Brandon over nothing.

"That's why he left me."

Rick's chest felt tight and he struggled to breathe. "So I'm not your nephew?" Even after everything she'd just told him, he needed to hear her say the words.

She reached across the table for his hands. "No, you're not my nephew, but I've always loved you with all my heart. Your grandparents do, too."

Rick kept shaking his head. "Why are you telling me now?"

"So that you know the truth. The DNA—"

"Get out."

Pamela flinched.

"Get the hell out of my house!" Rick snarled. He stood up so fast that his chair fell over with a loud crash. "Get the hell out!"

Pamela backed towards the door. "I'm sorry, Rickie. I never meant for any of this to happen."

"Get out!"

Duncan moved to Rick's side.

"I am sorry about everything, Rickie. Please don't hate me." She reached for the door handle. "Please."

Rick said nothing, just kept standing there with his hands clenched into fists at his sides.

As the door closed behind her, Duncan stepped closer to Rick. "It's going to be all right," he said.

Rick dragged his hands through his hair. "I'm not Rick Graham but I'm not Jefferson Newcastle either," he said. "So who the hell am I?"

Unable to resist, Duncan reached out and wrapped his arms around the other man.

Rick gripped back so tightly, Duncan thought his ribs might snap. But he didn't mind. *At least he isn't pushing me away.*

Rick inhaled sharply.

"You know in your heart who you are, and in the days ahead that will become a lot clearer."

"Maybe," Rick muttered.

"You just need some time. She's still your aunt."

"I can't forgive for this."

"You don't have too...but it will be your choice." Duncan hugged him more tightly. "You're not alone."

Chapter Sixteen

Duncan stumbled into his apartment and stripped off his sweaty tee-shirt. *Of all the days for the air in my car to break down,* he thought. *It* would *have to be the hottest day of the summer so far.* He headed towards the bathroom and unzipped his shorts.

The phone rang.

"Damn." Duncan eyed the shower, already imaging how refreshing the water would be, but only his business clients and his father would be calling him here.

"Duncan O'Neale," he said into the receiver.

"It's Elizabeth Newcastle. How're you doing?"

"I've been better," Duncan admitted to her. For some reason, he felt embarrassed about talking to her while dressed in just his boxers. "It's been a rather rough week."

"My brother?"

"Mostly. He had a barn burn down—no one was hurt, but I almost got roasted—and his aunt stopped by to visit today."

"Oh?"

"Yes, she wanted to clear the air about a few things." Duncan took a deep breath. "She confessed everything actually."

There was a gasp from over the phone. *"She did?"*

"It seems that the real Rick Graham died with his parents in that car wreck...and in her grief, the aunt stole a baby from the hospital nursery. She convinced herself that Jefferson was the real Rick and took him home with her. She flew him out to the grandparents. They never knew the truth." Duncan quickly spilled out the whole story.

"So it wasn't specifically Jefferson...it could have been any baby boy?"

"Yes."

"So why is she confessing this now?"

"Because Rick knows the truth from the DNA tests. She wanted his forgiveness."

"*I see.*"

Duncan could hear the anger in her voice. "Rick is taking it pretty hard. It's going to take a while for him to accept this."

"*And longer before he'll be ready to see me?*"

"I think so."

"*So what do you suggest that we do?*"

"We're going to have to wait. The only thing which will help Rick right now is giving him time to adjust." *Every time he starts to adapt, some new curve hits him.* "This is a big shock for him."

"*It is a shock for us all. All this time waiting to meet my brother...I can wait a bit longer, Mister O'Neale, but I will not be put off forever.*"

"I'm not asking you to wait forever," he told her, "but if we rush things, then he will bolt like one of his horses."

"*All right. I'm leaving this in your hands. Let me know when you can finally arrange a meeting.*"

"I will. Thank you."

* * *

Rick rode along the fence line. He was riding mechanically, not really paying attention to where he was going.

As he passed a small copse of trees which straddled the fence line, Jerry appeared on his side of the property. "Hey, Rick!"

Rick kept riding.

"Rick?" Jerry shouted it this time. "Whoa!"

Rick gave a start and jerked on the reins. "Oh, hi, Jerry."

"You got sunstroke or something?" Jerry dismounted from his own horse and climbed over the fence. "You ignoring me for a reason?"

"I was a little distracted."

"Oh no, buddy, you weren't even on this planet." Jerry pushed up the brim of his *Stetson*. "Where have you been? I've called you a few times today and got no answer. Not even your machine is on."

Rick just shook his head. "I've been out."

"Alone? Not riding with your private dick?" Jerry's leering grin quickly faded and he grimaced. "Is there something going on with you and the P.I. that I should know about?"

"I don't think so," Rick replied. "But then, I'm not too sure of anything at the moment."

"What kind of bullshit answer is that?"

"Oh, just wait until you hear the rest." Rick dismounted from his horse and looped the reins loosely around a tree branch. "Come on." He stepped deeper into the copse, out of the sun.

Jerry followed.

Sitting on the ground, Rick took a deep breath and then spilled the story Aunt Pamela had told him.

"Damn. That's fucking unbelievable." Jerry twirled his hat in his hand. "First your barn...and now this shit."

"Try being the cowboy on the end that fall."

"I'm sorry about this, Rick. I really am. Anything can I do?"

"No."

"You sure, buddy?"

"Yeah...just go home to your family."

"I'm not leaving you like this."

"We're not young, immature cowboys anymore. I have to handle this in my own way."

"Rick…"

Rick said nothing.

Jerry stood up, grimacing as he did so. "I'll go home, but I'll be back around to see you tomorrow." He didn't walk away, though. He wiped his hands off on his jeans. "Are you okay? I mean, really?"

Rick looked up at his friend. "I've taken a hard knock, but you know me better than anyone. I've had them before and I've survived. I'll survive this."

"But you don't have to do it alone."

"This time I have to."

"You don't. You have lots of friends." Jerry knew what he meant and they embraced before he slowly walked back to the fence.

Rick kept sitting under the trees.

She's still your aunt.

Duncan was right. Pamela was his aunt and Claudia was his granny. He couldn't wipe away those feelings, not even with the sense of indignation, betrayal and deception inside him. He wasn't Rick Graham. He couldn't seem to get beyond that or its implications.

Duncan said he knew who he was. Right now, he didn't. That would take time. Maybe forgiveness would, too.

* * *

Duncan opened his apartment door. "Rick!"

Rick looked terrible. He was unshaven and there were dark bags under his eyes. His shirt was rumpled and wrinkled and his jeans were dirty and stained. He was swaying slightly on his feet.

"Come in." Duncan practically pulled the other man inside. He could smell horse and other farm smells on him. *Exhausting yourself with work isn't the answer,* he thought.

"I've decided to forgive Pamela." Rick's voice was soft. "She wasn't in her right mind back then."

"I've been talking to Elizabeth Newcastle. I told her everything—it's only fair that she knows the truth too—and she's not going to press charges." Duncan paused. "She wanted to, at first, for kidnapping you. But she's not going to now," he added quickly. "There's no point in stirring up the past and dragging both of your families through the news."

"I was talking to Pamela on the phone....before I came here. We're not sure if we're going to tell Claudia."

Duncan nodded.

"And I need to meet this Elizabeth." Rick took a deep breath. "My—" his voice caught. "My sister."

"I'll make the arrangements."

"Thank you." Rick was still swaying.

"Are you all right?" Duncan asked him.

Rick looked at him. "Hold me?" he asked.

Duncan did so.

Also by Frank Sol

Novels Of The Sensual City
A Family Affair

Novels On The Prairies
Bareback Range
Return To Bareback Range
Fenced In